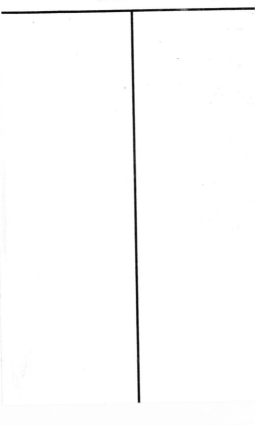

HIDDEN SYMPTOMS

HIDDEN SYMPTOMS

a novel by
DEIRDRE MADDEN

The Atlantic Monthly Press
BOSTON / NEW YORK

c. 2

First American Edition

LIBRARY OF CONGRESS CATALOGING-IN-PUBLICATION DATA

Madden, Deirdre.
  Hidden symptoms.

  Summary: After her brother's brutal murder, a twenty-
two-year-old university student in Belfast is torn by
her conflicting feelings of spirituality, as her religion
tortures more than comforts her.
  [1. Northern Ireland—Fiction] I. Title.
PR6063.A288H5   1986   823'.914   [Fic]   86-10753
ISBN 0-87113-065-3

                        BP

Printed in the United States of America

For my mother,
Mary Madden

HIDDEN
SYMPTOMS

of being antique, by which it would have proved that it had been beautiful for at least a hundred years, and therefore might well continue to be beautiful for years to come. She liked the egg, thought it to be beautiful, but could not say with conviction that that was how she would feel about it forever. And yet surely some things were absolutely beautiful: but why, and how did one recognize them?

Life became a series of evaluations and increasingly her confidence in her judgment was wavering, melting away, so that by this time only on things literary would she pass judgment with any degree of assurance. That assurance, at least, was still strong: the following afternoon, when asked for her opinion on an article which she had just finished reading, she did not hesitate to say firmly: "Trash."

The question was asked in a Belfast city-centre cafe, and the questioner, on entering, had noticed at first not Theresa, not that she was drinking tea and eating a doughnut, not even that she was dressed completely in black: he had noticed nothing except that she was reading a certain local "little magazine" and that there was a seat free at her table. He quickly sat down beside her, ordered a cup of coffee and as she turned the page smiled and said, "Good article, then?"

"Trash," she said firmly, taking a packet of cigarettes from her handbag and continuing to read.

"Oh," he said, deflated. "Why?"

"Because," she replied, waving a match to extinguish it, "it supports the view that Belfast, bombed, blitzed, beaten and bankrupt though it may be, is undergoing some sort of literary renaissance, that it is becoming a type of cultural omphalos, which I think is a nonsense. Badly written, too." She flicked ash into a little tin-foil ashtray, and her questioner seemed disgruntled.

"Lots being written," she admitted, "but this writer tries to compare it to the Irish Literary Renaissance. Cretin." She turned to look at the man beside her. He had, by this stage, noticed her dark clothes, dark hair, pale skin, her general angularity and her plain face, but he was taken aback by the large, brown eyes, which had a pronounced cast, so that even while she looked at him she seemed to be looking elsewhere. She wondered who this person was, with his two gold finger-rings and a very pronounced after-shave, who had looked so put out by her candour.

"Whose little boy are you, anyway?"

He took the magazine from her hand, turned to the head of the offending article, and pointed to the name: "Robert McConville." He was pleased to see that she went slightly red, but she shrugged her shoulders and said, "You've got a lot to learn then, haven't you?"

"And to what do you owe your great literary authority?" he sneered.

"I know a lot about literature," she said frankly. "I've read a great deal, and I can tell the difference between good writing and rubbish."

"Are you a writer, too?"

"No," she said, "I'm a student," and the expected sneer appeared on his lips. "Go on, then," she snapped, "boast to me of how little you know about literature, tell me how many times you failed your O-Level English — now which play is it that has Portia in it? — and yet it hasn't stopped you being a writer, has it; go on, give me all that, that's today's line, isn't it?"

"I have a degree in English from Queen's," he said, piqued.

"Then why smirk at me?" She ground out her cigarette, put her magazine in her bag and stood up.

"I'm sorry," he said, for she looked very angry and upset (although later he wondered why he had apologized, as it was she who had insulted him).

"Oh, forget it," she said, "it's foolish to argue over a little thing, I don't know why I did it. Excuse me, please," and, moving past him, she left the café.

Although it was late June, it was cool and overcast as Theresa returned home, and West Belfast looked bleak from the bus window. Had it been a city abroad, in France, say, or Germany, she would have been frightened, equating its ugliness with constant danger, but she could cope with Belfast, because she had watched it sink since her childhood from "normality" to its present state. She even found this new Belfast more acceptable than the city of her earliest memories, for the normality had always been forced, a prosperous facade over discrimination and injustice. Just as when she was small she had been very ill and the doctor diagnosed the illness as measles (for some reason the spots had failed to appear), Ulster before 1969 had been sick but with hidden symptoms. Streets and streets of houses with bricked-up windows and broken fanlights, graffiti on gable walls, soldiers everywhere: Belfast was now like a madman who tears his flesh, puts straws in his hair and screams gibberish. Before, it had resembled the infinitely more sinister figure of the articulate man in a dark, neat suit whose conversation charms and entertains; and whose insanity is apparent only when he says calmly, incidentally, that he will club his children to death and eat their entrails with a golden fork because God has told him to do so; and then offers you more tea.

She alighted from the bus two streets ahead of her usual stop, bought two fish suppers in the chip-shop and then hurried home, where her mother had plates and cutlery waiting by the hearth. The local news was beginning on television as they unrolled the greasy white packet and tipped chips onto the plates. The first item reported was the funeral of an RUC reservist who had been ambushed on his way to work earlier that week. Theresa, with a hot chip in her mouth, frowned and turned to BBC2 before the screen could show the flowers, the hearse, the coffin, the widow; she turned the sound down and they ate in silence, until her mother began to grumble about a visit which she was obliged to make that evening.

"Don't lie to me, you can't wait, you love every moment," said Theresa, and her mother groaned, for the lady whom she was to visit was struggling to bring up her children to be cultured. "Do your Shakespeare for Mrs. Cassidy, dear," she would say, and her ten-year-old son would obediently go down on one knee to declaim a portion of blank verse in a loud, ranting voice. "If I have to listen to thon' wee warthog playing 'The Merry Peasant' on the piano once more, I'll walk out, so I will. Boring old snob."

"Nice Mrs. Boomer. Clever little kiddies. Wish I was going. Give us a chip."

While her mother was preparing to leave, Theresa went upstairs to fetch a book. As she returned, she put her hand on the door-handle of her brother's room and paused, but she did not go in, descending instead to the parlour, where she passed the evening alone, reading, smoking and thinking.

Robert also had a duty visit to make that evening, to his sister and her family, the very sight of whose little red-brick terraced house always oppressed him and filled him with a powerful sense of the need to escape; a sense which was, in spite of its strength, vague, abstract, foolish even, when he seriously thought about it. For this had once been his home and he had escaped, he thought; he called only to please his sister, he called from free will and choice. If he really wanted, he need never go to that grim, narrow street ever again. Gloomily he rang the bell and his sister opened the door, beaming in delight when she saw him.

The whole family was at home: Rosie, her husband, Tom, who was watching television and nodded at his brother-in-law, "What about ye, Bobby" (Robert loathed abbreviations); and their little son, Tommy, who was playing with Lego on the floor. Rosie and Tom both hoped that the baby due in the autumn would be a little girl.

"Tea, Robert?" He refused but she insisted, heaving herself from the chair and shuffling into the kitchen. Tom said nothing. Robert rubbed his hands over his eyes and wanted to flee the place. He ran an eye around the room. Why were these houses so uniform? he wondered, looking at the brown-and-cream suite with wooden trim and the acrylic carpet with its busy pattern of abnormally large autumn leaves. Was there a working-class parlour in Belfast that lacked these fittings? A right tat palace this is, he thought. Above the fireplace was a huge picture in a broad plastic frame of a little boy with tears pouring down his cheeks, a work which should have appealed to none but sadistic pederasts. On the opposite wall was a large block print of Constable's "Haywain" with an excessively blue tint to it. In between were a string of horse brasses and two plates which had been there since before his mother died, one bearing a picture of Pope John XXIII and the other a picture of John F. and Jackie Kennedy. There was a sunburst clock of wood and metal and on the window-sill a clown of Murano glass. Tommy, still on the floor, was now sitting up eating liquorice torpedoes out of a crumpled bag. They look like pessaries, Robert thought dully, and shivered with vicarious nausea as the child slid another little torpedo into its plump, wet mouth. Rosie came back with a cup of tea and two Jaffa cakes for Robert just as the local news was beginning on television, and together they watched the funeral of the RUC reservist. "Good sauce for the bastard," said Tom, and Rosie frowned, looking at Tommy, but said nothing. She was sitting by the window, her head near to the gaudy glass clown, and as Robert drank his tea he watched her, wondering what it must be like to see the world through his sister's eyes, unable to empathize with the strange sensibility which could look around this room and perceive beauty; which could see aesthetic worth in, say, acid-green pampas grass.

"More tea, Robert?"

"Thanks."

When the main points of the news were over, they made conversation together, Rosie claiming that she felt fine. The doctors said that everything was alright and the only worry was that the summer would be a bit tiring, what with the heat and Tommy under her feet all day during the school holidays. Tommy himself said that Goldie, his pet fish, had died. He had made a wormery in the redundant round bowl, and Robert was obliged to go out to the back scullery to see these new pets, visible at intervals between the soil and the glass. Rosie told him innocent gossip about neighbors whom he had almost forgotten through absolute indifference; he said that his work was going well, Tom talked sport and at seven o'clock Robert had fulfilled his duty and left.

After such visits, Robert always liked to go straight back to his flat, which was near the university. There was, he thought, a smell in his sister's house: not a bad smell, but the smell of people and cheap food: a smell of poverty. He felt it clinging to his clothes and skin, and he removed it immediately on his return with a hot shower and lots of male toiletries which smelt bitter, sexy and expensive. As he dried himself afterwards, Count Basie on stereo, he took comfort in looking around his flat at his possessions: the pale wicker furniture, his French theatre posters and a cunning little water-colour of two deck chairs. In his heart of hearts he despised himself for gaining any sort of peace and comfort from such trivia, but their power as symbols of successful escape from the squalor that was home was, to him, undeniable.

I love my squint, thought Theresa, as she tried to gaze at herself in the mirror late that night. The man in the café had seemed distinctly disconcerted by it. It was hers alone, untraceable to any ancestor, unlike her nose and legs, which she had inherited from her mother as definitively as one might make a grandfather clock and a pair of Meissen candlesticks. She found it slightly weird to look at her mother's First Communion photograph, where the little sepia legs below the frock of white watered silk had just such an artful kink in them as her own legs did. Hamlet, I am thy Father's spirit, an' begob it was an' all, for you could tell the young fella off the Da by the nose on him. People even said that she looked like her grandmother, who had died before Theresa was born, and vestiges of that dead face were then looking back at her from her own reflection. How strange and arbitrary it all seemed to be, people marrying, mating and mixing genes; unavoidable choice and chance producing cocktails of children with inherited traits and yet still new people with their own particularities, like Theresa's squint. She wished suddenly that her father had not died when she was so very young.

I'll probably meet again that man whom I insulted, she thought as she got into bed. Belfast was so small, incestuous almost, in the way paths crossed. And she hated that; she was still bumping into people who sympathized with her, Oh that's the girl, even once or twice on introduction they remembered or at least conjectured, you could see it in their eyes. Only one of hundreds and the case short, obscure: what of those whose losses were famous and had made the English papers, *Newsweek*, history?

A light summer rain beat softly on the window. So little mattered. The temptation to make one's response as big as the disaster had to be resisted, for in truth what could one do, save collapse down to the horror of little details and keep living? She had read somewhere that there was a museum to the Holocaust in Israel, and that one of the exhibits was a tiny broken shoe upon a pedestal. "But what can we *do*?" Inexorable time: often it was truly too late to do anything.

A mere two days later she had her comeuppance. While browsing in a bookshop she was brightly accosted by Kathy, who was her only friend from Queen's, and beside her stood the insulted journalist.

"Hello, Theresa, are you buying, or just looking? Do you know my boyfriend, Robert? He's a writer." Theresa smiled at both definitions, made with such pitiful firmness and pride.

Robert grimaced. "We met a few days ago, in a café. Theresa didn't think much of my last article."

"Well, it wasn't very good, now, was it, Robert?" said Kathy firmly. "In all honesty, you have written much better. He's compiling a book now," she added to Theresa, "a directory of Northern Irish writers. It'll be very comprehensive."

"How interesting," said Theresa politely, fixing her strange eyes upon the writer and smiling. He stared back coldly. Kathy, while grumbling about having to remain in Belfast during the entire summer, removed a pen and a little notebook from her handbag. "Come and see us next Tuesday," she said, leaning on a pile of Royal biographies to scrawl down the address. "Seven o'clock, I'll make dinner."

"Thank you," said Theresa, taking the proffered little page. She smiled again at Robert and this time he smiled back, but thinly.

Theresa was glad to see that the address given was evidently that of Robert's flat, and not of Kathy's home in Harberton Park, where she lived with her mother. Theresa's confidence, vacillating when concerned with anything save matters literary, became suddenly and surprisingly firm when faced with the phenomenon of Mrs. O'Gorman. In short, she had the lady nailed, and on the strength of one brief meeting would have said that Mrs. O'Gorman was a ghastly woman with the same conviction with which she would have affirmed that *Ulysses* was a good book.

The account of Paddy Dignam's funeral in *Ulysses* always brought Kathy to Theresa's mind. When she read of the unidentified figure by the grave whom a reporter later erroneously named as "McIntosh" (because the unknown gentleman was wearing one), she always thought of her friend who, at college, by simple non-appearance at lectures and tutorials, made a mystery of herself. Kathy who? Her very sex was in question: a notice pleading for an essay appeared on the departmental noticeboard for a Mr. O'Gorman, written by a tutor who thought that the K. O'Gorman who was on his class list but who had attended no tutorials was a lazy young man instead of a lazy young woman. Meanwhile, Kathy's presence was adding sparkle to parties, plays, concerts, wine bars and bedsits: she was in evidence everywhere but the Arts library. She made it a point of honour to read as few of the set books as possible, preferring in their stead things obscure, obscene, quaint and curious, so that she had read *Barrack-Room Ballads*, but not *The Prelude*; *Fanny Hill*, but not *Wuthering Heights*; and *The Tibetan Book of the Dead*, but not *King Lear*. She also kept an astute eye on the Belfast cultural scene and in conversation would make claims to the friendship of writers, artists and actors with whom, in reality, she was merely acquainted. Possibly her only sincere friendship was with Theresa, who cared nothing for Kathy's considerable prowess as a social climber but who was immensely fond of the kindhearted and sensible person whom she perceived under the exuberant exterior.

In the summer exams every year, Kathy would scrape

a minimal pass, dependent always on the copious notes which Theresa gave her to photocopy and cram. It was through the operation of this favour that Theresa had the misfortune to meet Kathy's mother.

Kathy and Theresa never socialized in each other's homes at Theresa's implicit request, and so when she went to Harberton Park one day to retrieve some lecture notes which she needed urgently, it was the first time that she had ever seen the large, elegant detached house which was the O'Gorman home. As Theresa ascended the steps, the mirthful sounds of half a conversation were audible through the open door, drowned suddenly by a peal of barks, both deep and shrill, as three dogs rushed out of the house and began woofing and snapping at her ankles. One was a Dalmatian, one an Afghan hound, and one an ugly little thing with a mashed face, like a genetically defective cat; and all three barked constantly, the Dalmatian jumping up and putting its large paws on her skirt. She was too shocked to run or scream and only realized how frightened she was when a fourth bark joined in: "Toby! Prince! Down, boy!" Mrs. O'Gorman called off the two larger dogs and scooped up the ugly little one in a jewelled hand. "Who are you?" she snapped. "What do you want?"

"Kathy, please," said Theresa weakly, conscious mainly of the blood booming in her ears, and the startled beats of her heart.

"She's not in."

"Poetry notes," Theresa whimpered, and the woman turned her back and went into the house, returning a moment later with the tatty folder of yellow cardboard which contained almost everything Theresa had ever learnt about Augustan poetry.

"Thank you," she said, but she was talking to air. The woman had gone and the telephone conversation was resumed. Theresa left quickly, for the two large dogs were still on the top step, panting and slavering hungrily.

Kathy later apologized for her absence.

"You did get the notes?"

"Yes," said Theresa, too embarrassed to elaborate, although she soon discovered that such conduct was not without precedent. Mrs. O'Gorman was an ill-mannered snob who treated her daughter with scant regard, much less her daughter's friends, and so Kathy tried to keep friends and mother as far apart as possible. Although the two lived together, it was in a constant state of acrimony. Kathy was an only child: she told Theresa that her father had died when she was a baby and she had an inferiority complex about her lack of family life.

For a long time after the incident with the dogs, Theresa had a perverse fascination with the event. Such conduct in a mother was so strange. Common sense told Theresa that being a mother did not automatically free one of ill-temper and boorishness, and so of course she knew that it was wrong of her to use her own mother as a rule-of-thumb for the world — as wrong as it was irresistible. Everyone could only but be found wanting.

One day, years previously, a hoary old man named Harry, six foot two and with hands like a mole, had come to do odd jobs in the house, and when Theresa returned from school she saw in the kitchen a plateful of enormous scones, each one about four inches across.

"Sufferin' Isaac, Ma, what's wrong with the scones? Did you lose the small cutter?"

But her mother had replied no, that their size was intentional, because she had made them for Harry and she had thought that big scones would be easier for him to manage than dainty little normal ones. Theresa always remembered setting down her school-bag and gazing at the scones with something approaching reverence. Universal love on a thick delft plate with puce roses: she had thought then, "I shall never be better than this, I shall never be anywhere nearly as good." Thoughtfulness to the humble level of an old man's dexterity in eating scones. Never neglect the little things in life. The rest of the poor world could only fall short.

(Mrs. O'Gorman fell further than most: Theresa imagined her forcing Harry to eat his own sandwiches outside. In a thunderstorm.)

The day before the dinner party, Theresa phoned Kathy.

"You are coming, aren't you?"

"Yes, of course, Kathy." She paused nervously. "Kathy, you haven't told your friend about Francis yet, have you?"

"Who, Robert? No, not yet," she replied.

"Well, don't," said Theresa quickly. "I mean, I'd rather you didn't. I — it's hard to explain — I hardly know why — "

"Forget it," said Kathy's voice, disembodied and kindly.

"He'll never hear about it from me, if that's the way you want it: I promise."

"Thank you. Thank you very much indeed."

"No problem. See you and your appetite tomorrow at seven. Don't forget now. 'Bye."

Theresa replaced the receiver, feeling foolish. It was almost as if she were ashamed of what had happened. Anyway, she thought bitterly, who cared now except her mother and herself? Who else had ever truly cared?

The evening evolved strangely. Theresa brought a bottle of Blue Nun and complimented Robert on his flat. "It says a lot about you."

"Thank you," he said, genuinely pleased, not sensing the irony. The room screamed of the persona he had created for himself: short of whitewashing the walls and writing I AM AN INTELLECTUAL in large red letters, it could not have been made to "say" more. Kathy, in a dress of burgundy velvet with an antique lace collar, served out a vegetable stew which they ate with brown rice as an accompaniment and the Chieftains as background music.

"We'll have to go over to Queen's in a week or two to collect our exam results," Kathy said. "It's barbaric, pinning them up like that. It reminds me of those old B-movies about Oxford, jostling to see if you got through: 'It's beastly luck, Carruthers, Mater'll be so disappointed at my being sent dhine.' God, I wonder if I'll make it again this year?"

Robert said that exams were always a temptation to

destruction for him: he had been fascinated by the simplicity with which he could undo a year's study, just as when, on a clifftop or at a high window, he was attracted by how simply his life could be ended. "One little step forward and I die. If I leave this room and do something utterly mundane for the next three hours — browse in a bookshop or eat sausage rolls in the Union — I can quickly end forever my university career."

Theresa agreed. Exams inspired her, too, with a feeling of awesome power rather than of knowledge. They talked about the university and about literature until the door was aggressively knocked and a friend of Robert's entered, uninvited and inebriated, his eagerness to contribute to the conversation equalled only by his thirst. He was a struggling playwright with manic eyes and a belligerent manner.

"You," he said, taking the glass of Blue Nun offered by Kathy and stabbing his finger at Theresa. "D'you write plays, you?"

"No," she said, "but I write lots of prose." (Something which Robert had not known until then.)

"Prose is nothin'. Prose is useless. Ye ought to write plays. Plays is the only useful art."

"Useful? In what way?"

"Useful! Bloody useful! D'ye know what useful means, even? Plays are social, they're about people, so they are, you get things done with plays. People see themselves on a stage and then they know," he added mysteriously.

The discussion became intense thereafter.

The newcomer drank all the wine at an amazing rate

and Theresa deliberately baited him, saying flatly, "Drama is the bastard child of literature," and "Drama is, of all art forms, the most unsatisfactory and the most inferior." Robert was amused by her total coolness while, visibly tongue-in-cheek, she drove the playwright almost to tears of anger and frustration, and each statement was a goad, calculated, and honed to cruel sharpness before being lunged with heartless success at its target. When Robert tried to join in, the playwright told him to shut his bake, he was only a critic, what did he know; later he asked Robert where he had dug up this "bourgeoise hoor" (Robert, oddly, thought at first that he meant Kathy), and eventually told them all that they were a pack of fascists before lurching off drunkenly, taking the empty wine bottle with him.

"Oooh, that was funny," said Kathy, as Robert sat a bowl of fruit before them. "He's a lot less interesting when he's sober, but he's rarely that."

"He's decent enough," said Robert, "just a terrible bigot."

"That's not what's wrong with him," replied Theresa. "It's the direction his bigotry takes. All great writers were bigoted — Joyce and his like — but bigoted about their art. If writers get too obsessed with other things, like politics or the state of the world, their art becomes less important to them. Your man doesn't take his plays seriously enough. He only thinks of them as tools to serve some end, not as ends in themselves, and the plays suffer; they're bound to." She took up an orange and began to peel it. "Fascists, indeed; he's a half-fascist himself for all that talk of 'the people.' He judges too much, he wants to change things, change people. This is wrong and this is wrong, I say so, I say that it must be changed and this is how. If he had any intelligence and ability, he'd be downright dangerous."

"Aren't all great social reformers just as you've described him?" asked Robert.

"All great dictators, rather. What is a dictator, anyway, but a misguided social reformer? And an artist is something different again."

"And what's that?"

"An artist," she said, "is a person who composes or paints or sculpts or writes."

"Oh, come on, Theresa," said Kathy, who was lying on the floor languidly chewing an apple. "That's a rather elitist view, isn't it?"

"No, I don't think so — just rather traditional. People like your man make it sound very easy to be an artist. I think that it must be difficult — very difficult indeed."

"What do you write about?" Robert asked. Theresa waited for a few moments before answering, and when she did she looked at him in a calculating manner, as if to register the effect which each word had upon him. It made him doubt her sincerity.

"I write about subjectivity — and inarticulation — about life pushing you into a state where everything is melting until you're left with the absolute and you can find neither the words nor the images to express it."

"It sounds frightening."

"It is."

[28]

"I don't understand that," said Kathy.

"It doesn't matter," said Theresa, suddenly brisk. "It's late, I must go home." They had difficulty in persuading her to stay, and eventually she remained only for a quick cup of coffee; she then thanked them and left.

Kathy and Robert remained in the flat, cradling their warm, empty coffee cups in their hands and listening to the soft music of the stereo. It was a long time before Robert spoke.

"Kathy?"

"Yes?"

He stroked her head as one might stroke a cat.

"Are you going home tonight?"

She raised herself up from the floor and he leaned down from his chair; she kissed him and said, "No," pulled herself up to his lap, kissed him again and said that if her mother was not used to unannounced absences by now, then she ought to be; then kissed him long and deeply, sighed and murmured in his ear that she loved him. He did not believe this, but he kissed her back.

They made love and Robert lay awake for a long time after Kathy had fallen asleep beside him. He tried to understand what Theresa had been getting at when she spoke of subjectivity: he could think only of evil and violence. He was not sure that he understood anything about evil, but by God it was easy to assimilate! Every day he could take huge mysterious lumps of evil into his consciousness and the only worrying result was that he did not worry. That very day he had been upstairs in a bus which had been overtaken by a lorry carrying meat from the knacker's yard. For well over two miles he had looked down into the tipper, which was full of skinned limbs: long, bloody jawbones; jointed, whip-like tails. It had been a horrendous sight, but he had not averted his eyes from the mobile shambles: he had gazed unflinchingly down into it. This was how things were. He had looked at so many ugly and evil things, unsubtle as a lorryload of dead meat, and he had said in his heart that this was how things were. He had accepted that lorry. He accepted too much.

He remembered television news reports, where the casual camera showed bits of human flesh hanging from barbed wire after a bombing. Firemen shovelled what was left of people into heavy plastic bags, and you could see all that remained: big burnt black lumps like charred logs. And he could look at such things and be shocked and eat his tea and go out to the theatre and forget about it. He could cope when it did not involve him personally. Now he found himself wondering how he would feel if it was Kathy whose flesh was hanging from barbed wire in thin, irregular strips and shifting in the wind like surreal party streamers. How would he feel if the soft little body beside him was to be translated into an anonymous black lump and shovelled into a plastic bag? He tried to tell himself that it was only a ghoulish thought, but he knew that for so many people this sudden change was a reality in the people whom they slept with, ate with, lived with and loved, and his own lack of empathy saddened him. In the darkness he touched

Kathy's sleeping shoulder, and suddenly felt as lonely as Adam.

Gently he awoke her, kissed her and stroked her; whispered lies in her ear. She murmured and giggled, half-awake and half-sleeping. He desperately wanted to bury his fearful loneliness in the blackness of the room and in her thin, warm body, but sex solved nothing: there was only panic and the illusion of union; nothing could protect him. Now he hated himself for having visited his morbid thoughts of violent death upon this innocent person beside him, for he had not really been thinking about her, nor even about how much her death would mean to him. He was afraid that his own innocent body might be destroyed violently and quickly and he had been too cowardly even to imagine such a thing, visiting his fear upon Kathy instead. Suddenly, incredibly, he wanted to cry.

"Robert? Robert?"

But he did not answer her and he did not cry, because he was ashamed and embarrassed and he did not love her.

They kept lumber up in the attic and Theresa found there, on the day after the dinner party, a dead Red Admiral caught in a cobweb. Other cobwebs were spun in arcs across the windowpane, catching the sunlight in their fine rainbow strands. Mentally, she recited a fragment of poetry which she had learnt for her exams:

> *Upon the dusty glittering windows cling,*
> *And seem to cling upon the moonlit skies*

[31]

Tortoiseshell butterflies, peacock butterflies,
A couple of nightmoths are on the wing.
Is ever modern nation like the tower,
Half dead at the top?

She half-remembered a legend from somewhere which said that butterflies were the souls of the dead. She touched a little wing with the tip of a finger and some of the bright colour dusted off; the brittle corpse shifted in the web. "The souls of the virtuous are in the hands of the LORD and no torment shall ever touch them."

She sat on the edge of the tin trunk and wished that she could talk with Francis, for she wished him to help clarify a dream which she had had the preceding night. It concerned the school which they had both attended as children and, with the weird particularity common to dreams, the dominant feature had been the school's radiators, covered with chipped magenta paint and always tepid. Above the radiators were tiled window-sills, ranged along with pots of geraniums. The dream had been so vivid that she had even seen and heard the grit of the soil grate between the pots and the saucers placed beneath them to catch the drips. She had also glimpsed, briefly, the overall layout of the school, and on waking she had been puzzled, for she had dreamt of doors and windows in places which she sensed were not quite right, and now she could not remember what the school had really looked like. Was her waking memory accurate, or had the dream been the truth rising to the surface now after the passing of years? Everything was confused: never again would she be able to picture the school to herself with any confidence; now all was a jumble of dream and supposed reality. And never again could she ask Francis for confirmation or clarification, because Francis was dead. She was alone now, and at the mercy of her own memory and imagination.

Perched on the edge of the tin trunk, she began to cry for him as she had not cried for a very long time, reflexively, almost; she could not stop herself and it hardly occurred to her to try. And while the body cried (the eyes wept, the mouth wailed and the fists tried to wipe away the tears), her mind seemed independent of this spontaneous grief. Something within her, calm and apparently rational, was thinking that it was impossible for her to continue living without him, that she needed him as she needed air. She did not believe that she could bear the loneliness of being in this world without him.

Such absolute loneliness had come to her the first night after his death, when she went to bed. Lights out, she put her head down and then, too, she had started to cry automatically. When they were children, she had fingered the pink satin bindings on the edge of the blankets until they were frayed and split; and Francis, before sleeping, had plaited the fringes of the rug. Always for her to be in bed in a dark room was to be in a place timeless as the sea. Now she lay under those same blankets and rugs and a cold stiff sheet, but everything had changed. The fact of his death was something which she would have to take to bed with her for the rest of her life, a new reality which ended innocence as absolutely as lost virginity; ineluctable, irreversible. On waking, his death would still be there. For every moment of every day until she also died, his death would be there, and if she forgot about it for a moment, a week, a year, even if it were possible for her to put it from her mind forever, it would not change the truth. His death would still always be there, waiting silently to be recognized and remembered.

When she had stopped crying, she lit a cigarette and while she smoked it tried to control her thoughts. It was dangerous to think too much about his having been murdered: that was to risk being lost in bitterness and hate. She tried to make herself think only of the pain of loss: that in itself was enough.

When she had finished her cigarette she brushed some ash from her knee, and left the attic.

Three days later, Robert received a brief, polite letter thanking him for a most interesting and enjoyable evening. That afternoon, on emerging from the revolving doors of the Central Library, he discovered the writer of the letter standing on the top step, her irregular eyes narrowed in concentration as she lit a cigarette.

"You'll kill yourself with those things," he said.

"Good," she said, after a slight pause, looking at him sideways. He said that his car was parked nearby and he offered her a lift home.

"Are you going towards West Belfast?" she asked.

"Yes, I'm going to see my sister. I can leave you off."

She thanked him and they walked to the car together. When her cigarette was finished she immediately lit another. She spoke little. He wondered if she was shy, and as he drove up the Falls Road he glanced over at her and decided she was most definitely not.

"You must meet Rosie," he said with insincere warmth as he turned into the street where his sister lived, thinking that the encounter might be revealing.

Unlike Robert, however, Theresa did not react with perceptible revulsion to the vulgarity which came out to meet them at a front door bristling with knobs, knockers, brass numbers and bell-pulls. She did not start at the sheer ugliness of the living-room and, although he cringed at Rosie's attitude of good hostess, she did not.

Only Rosie and little Tommy were at home. The latter lay sleeping on the sofa, one arm stretched out Romantically and the other clasping a tatty cuddly toy: the dead Chatterton with a Womble. Rosie shook him awake to meet the visitor and, smitten with shyness, he stuck his face in his mother's armpit.

"Come on now, none of that. Show Theresa the good boy you are. Do Shakin' Stevens for her." From her apron pocket she produced a ten-pence piece as a bribe. "Go on, Tommy, do Shakin' Stevens for her. Go on, do Shakey." She waved the coin enticingly before his nose and a pudgy, covetous fist shot out to grab the money, but she raised her hand higher. "No, Tommy, only when you've done Shakey for Theresa." His eyes flickered sadly. He was torn between timidity and greed, but timidity won out and he would not perform.

Rosie went into the kitchen to make tea and took Theresa with her, while Robert eavesdropped shamelessly from the living-room . Their conversation centered around the object which Robert probably hated more than any other in the house: a small plaque which hung over the sink and incorporated a stump of grey plastic to represent the Madonna, a few flowers of coloured tin, and the words "A la Grotte Benie j'ai prié pour toi." He could hear Rosie saying that if her Premium Bond came up she would go to Lourdes; she had always wanted to, but unless she won something it would be years and years before she could ever afford it. And to his amazement, the Basilisk was heard to reply that she had always wanted to go to Lisieux because her real name was Marie Therese; she was called for the Little Flower.

Robert at this point congratulated himself on having brought her to the house. This was a new side altogether! Little Flower! He almost snorted aloud in scorn. Then he heard his sister's voice say very softly, "Robert doesn't practise his religion any more. It's very sad, he got sort of — cynical — as he grew up."

"Oh, that often happens," he heard Theresa answer airily. "People read things and they get fancy ideas in their heads; they think they know it all. He'll grow out of it."

"I doubt it," said Rosie solemnly. "He's twenty-eight now."

And Robert was furious to realize immediately on Theresa's re-entering the room (although she gave him neither grin nor glance to intimate this) that she had known all along he was listening in, and that her last remark was a deliberate gibe to which he could not reply without revealing that he had been ear-wigging.

For a long time after that, every time he saw a flower or heard one mentioned he grimaced to think how inappropriate a symbol it was for his angular and defensive friend. To savour fully its absurdity, he stopped one day before a florist's window in Royal Avenue, where the display of blooms was exact and exotic as a Rousseau jungle; and Robert started in surprise when a florist's face suddenly appeared through the foliage, bright as a naif tiger. She removed a green tin vase of Baby's Breath and retired, but her action had exposed to Robert a much more significant vase. It contained bunches of Tiger Lilies, magnificent in their beauty and perfection, and yet when Robert looked at them closely they unnerved him. From the heart of every flower started long, whip-like stamens, each terminating in a blunt, dark and dusty anther. The thick, creamy-white petals were prickled slightly towards the centre of each flower and the fleshy points were stippled bright red, as if with blood. He imagined a heavy, cloying perfume. If she were any sort of flower, he thought, this was it: not a soft, sweet-smelling innocent little blossom, but this bloody, savage, phallic, heartless flower. He thought of how incessantly she smoked, and wondered why he found her so frightening.

At Robert's mother's wake, seemingly countless women with tired faces who were fresh from kissing her corpse and touching their Rosary beads to her hands had grasped Robert by the forearm and quavered, "Your mother was a saint, son." His mother died when he was twenty-two, his father having long predeceased her, dying when Robert was eight. Sometimes it bemused him to think how slight the effect of that first death had been upon him, and how faint were his memories of his father; so faint that, ludicrously, he even wondered at times if he had imagined him. Outside a Christian Fundamentalist Church on the Donegal Pass, he had once misread the words of their Wayside Pulpit and saw on the virulent pink poster not "Have You Ever Thought Of God As Your Father?" but "Have You Ever Thought Of Your Father As God?" And in a strange vision the God in whom he did not believe became one with his father, whose existence he also doubted. The unreal Supreme Being flashed across his mind as a mild little Belfast man with a loft full of pigeons and a weak heart. People also praised him highly after his death. "He'd have given ye two ha'pennies for a penny, your Da."

As Robert grew up he found it increasingly difficult to live with his mother. He did not understand her. He did not understand the strange, intense religion which dominated her life. He had no patience with her saints, her statues, her novenas, her holy pictures, her holy water, her blind, total, absolute faith. As a child, he had disliked religion because it made him feel guilty and he became increasingly disenchanted as he grew up. By the time he left school he did not believe in God, nor did he want to.

He was a total disappointment to his mother, rejecting both her religion and the petit bourgeois aspirations which she nurtured on his behalf. She wanted him to marry a nice Catholic girl from a decent Catholic family; a teacher or nurse, for choice. She wanted him to "get on," to get a good steady job, and although she was pleased that he went to university his choice of subject — English Literature — dismayed her. Although uneducated herself, she was astute enough to know that an arts degree was not an instant passport to a highly remunerative or socially acceptable career. He refused to study law, refused teacher training, refused to apply for a clerical post with the Civil Service. And although all this vexed her a great deal, perhaps they could have muddled along with minimal acrimony had it not been for Robert's total lack of religion.

"What does it profit a man if he gain the whole world but lose his soul?" How often had she said that to him? She believed that everyone had their own particular cross to bear in life and he was obviously hers. Sometimes she looked as though she actually had to carry all six foot two and twelve stone of him around on her frail and narrow back. Her face was tired and sad during their habitual disagreements, but only once had she lost her temper and that was on the unforgettably embarrassing day when, in the course of tidying his room, she found a packet of contraceptives. When he came in that evening she faced him with it, and he saw that she was deeply shocked: her own son was a damned soul, an evil and wicked person. What she had found proved his perdition to her as conclusively as a box of black tallow candles.

Robert's memory operated in a cruel and unfortunate manner, clouding his happy memories and sharpening the unhappy; and so when he thought, reluctantly, of scenes which he would rather forget — scenes of pain and anger and embarrassment and grief — they always returned to him in absurdly vivid detail. He could still feel the terrible cringing shame of that moment when he walked in and saw the offending packet sitting at the extreme edge of the kitchen table, as far away as was possible from half a black-crusted bap swathed in tissue paper and a bone-handled knife, smeared with butter and jam to its hilt. He saw the wedding ring bedded into the red flesh of his mother's hand, which trembled with what he perversely imagined to be fear: he was genuinely surprised when she flared out angrily.

"Aren't you the big fella, eh? Aren't you the smart lad? Will ye be so smart if some of yer lady friends has a baby? Then what'll ye do?"

"Oh, come on, Ma," he had mumbled, "the whole point is that they won't have babies."

At this she lost her temper completely and began to hit him, her anger immense but her blows pathetically weak and puny. With one short, effortless movement of his arm he could have shoved her out into the back scullery to cool off in the company of the mangle, a red net sack of Spanish onions and a meat safe, but he could not bring himself to do it. Instead, he stood there gormlessly while she hit him, and wished that her thumps were more powerful and painful and worthy of resistance. At last, worn out, she started to cry and left the kitchen: he could hear her sobbing as she clumped upstairs to her room.

Home life was extremely frosty for a very long time after that and the eventual thaw was never complete: they were never on the same footing again. She still railed at him frequently for being irreligious and immoral, but never again referred to the row or its cause. They were more polite to each other than they had been before. He was quite surprised that she did not insist upon his leaving home; in fact, when he broached the delicate question one day, she said disarmingly, "Why would ye do that? D'ye think I'd put me own flesh an' blood out on the streets?"

"I'd get a flat," he said foolishly.

"Ye've no money," was her pragmatic reply. "Ye'll be time enough when ye're earning."

The following year, Rosie married and Tom moved in, Robert left university, started working for a local arts magazine and moved out. But he was under no illusions. He always knew what his mother thought she was up against, and she developed a way of looking at him that made him shiver. She saw him as damned but not past redemption, and his lack of the desire to be redeemed was a real torment to her.

She died almost a year after Rosie's marriage. On the day she was hospitalized, Robert was sitting by her bed when she opened her eyes and gazed vaguely around the ward.

"Ma," he whispered, "it's me, Robert. Is there anything I can do for you?" And she had slid her tired, watery eyes sideways, looking at him with ridicule and pity. As if he needed to ask what she wanted of him! He was spoiling her death; he was the unfinished business she would take to her grave. He hoped she realized that she was not responsible for whatever was wrong in him. Did she know that people who didn't believe in God (and who didn't want to — could she understand that?) — such people could not change to belief at a moment's notice merely to oblige their mothers.

But she had looked away again, closed her eyes and three hours later became comatose, remaining thus for three more days, at the end of which time she died.

Theresa's mother stretched up and ripped off a little page from the wad of months stitched together beneath a reproduction of Murillo's "Flight into Egypt." "First of July," she said, scrunching up June in her fist. "Feast of the Holy Blood." Theresa warmed the teapot and tossed two tea bags into it; her mother threw the crumpled page into the fire and then glanced over the list of feasts for the new month. "Our Francis was a martyr, wasn't he?" she said.

"I suppose he was," Theresa replied, "but he had no choice, had he?"

"What do you mean?"

"I mean martyrs usually have a choice; if they deny their religion they're allowed to live, and if they won't deny it, well, they martyr them. And they just killed Francis because of his religion, he had no choice."

"How do you know?" said her mother.

She paused. "Well, yes," she said, "you're right, I don't. We don't know anything at all about what happened to him, only that . . . I suppose he was a martyr."

She made the tea, poured it out and they drank it without speaking. Theresa also had a cigarette to calm herself, angry at having set up that little exchange. Such talk reminded them of how very little they knew of the circumstances in which Francis had died. Once, while reading a terrorist court case in the paper, her mother had said, "Maybe when they catch the person who killed our Francis, we'll find out more," but Theresa found the thought of this horrifying. Unlike her mother, who was haunted by the idea of the "someone" who had killed her son, Theresa could hardly believe that such a person existed. Only on two occasions had she been completely convinced of the reality of Francis's murderer, and she had found it overwhelming.

It first happened shortly after his death, when she awoke from a nightmare in the small hours one morning and realized that just as it would be impossible to find Francis now, no matter where in the city or the world one went, so also it would be impossible not to find somewhere the man who had killed him. That person was somewhere out there as surely as she was in bed in her room, and his invisible existence seemed to contaminate the whole world. She lay awake until morning, afraid to sleep in the darkness which contained him.

A few days after that, she arrived too early for an arranged meeting with Kathy in a city-centre pub. She bought a drink and while she waited she looked around at the the other customers, the majority of whom were men, until slowly the thought of the man who had killed her brother crept back into her mind. Those men who were laughing over in the corner; that man with reddish hair and big, rough hands who was drinking alone; even the white-coated barman, cutting wedges of lemon for gin-and-tonics: any one of them might have done it. She gazed at each of them in turn and thought in cold fright: "Is he the one? Did he do it? Is he the man who murdered Francis?" It was, of course, improbable, but it was possible, and that grain of possibility took away the innocence of every man in the pub, and of every man whom she would ever see in the city. Every stranger's face was a mask, behind which Francis's killer might be hiding. The barman approached the table and said, "Will I get you another drink?" She could not bear to raise her eyes to look at him, but shook her bowed head in refusal of his services. From that day on, Belfast was poisoned for her. She could not conceive of Francis's killer as an individual, as a person who might be arrested, tried and punished, but only as a great darkness which was hidden in the hearts of everyone she met. It was as if the act of murder was so dreadful that the person who committed it had forfeited his humanity and had been reduced to the level of pure evil. He had dragged that world down with him: everyone was guilty.

It was a hot day. She took another cup of tea and a cigarette out to the back yard, a tiny flagged area where a few drab flowers grew in tubs between the dustbin and the coalhouse. The smoke trailed up from the cigarette between her fingers like a fine filament of grey silk. She slitted her eyes and looked up at the bright sky. All of July to get through. All of August. All of September. All of her life.

At the beginning of July, Theresa and Kathy's examination results were released. They met in the city centre and walked out nervously together to the university, found their names on the boards and then went to Robert's flat.

"Crack the Bollinger," said Kathy gleefully when she opened the door. "I made it again, albeit by a whisker. Needless to say, Theresa here breezed through." They went inside and Robert produced a bottle of cheap sparkling wine. "Not Bollinger, but the best I can manage," he said.

"It'll do," said Kathy. "Keep the vintage stuff for the finals."

He opened the wine and while they drank Kathy happened to mention the flags and bunting which they had seen up along Sandy Row in preparation for the Twelfth.

"I think that the way in which society tolerates the Orange Order is ridiculous," said Theresa. "I mean, they even encourage them by televising their tasteless marches. Can you imagine the National Front or the neo-Nazis being treated like that? Can't you just hear the television commentary? 'And the sun is smiling down today on the men of the Ku Klux Klan.' "

"Oh, come on, Theresa," said Robert, "that's a bit strong. The Twelfth processions are not that bad. They're just a bit of folk culture. They are vulgar, I'll grant you that, but surely it's best to let them march; isn't it harmless that way?"

"Harmless? You seem to forget, Robert," she said stiffly, "that the Orange Order is, first and foremost, an anti-Catholic organization. They hate Catholics, Robert, and hate is never harmless. It worries me that intelligent Protestants can't see that, but when it bypasses an intelligent Catholic then I'm no longer worried, I'm afraid."

"I'm not a Catholic," he said shortly, and was startled by the vehemence of her reply.

"Oh, come on, Robert," she snapped, "spare me that. I know your background and it's about as Catholic as you can get."

"But I don't believe in Catholicism. I don't even believe in God. Religion's a lot of eyewash as far as I'm concerned."

Theresa laughed cynically. "Just tell me this: if you were found in the morning with a bullet in your head, what do you think the papers would call you? An agnostic? No, Robert, nobody, not even you, is naive enough to think that. Of course you don't believe: but there's a big difference between faith and tribal loyalty, and if you think that you can escape tribal loyalty in Belfast today you're betraying your people and fooling yourself."

Kathy was startled to see the turn which the conversation had taken, but already it had gone too far for her to stop it.

"Christ, Theresa, with people like you around it's no wonder the country's in the state it's in," said Robert.

"And if we were all like you it would be a right little

Utopia, wouldn't it? You must have really enjoyed life under the Stormont Government. Do you feel like a second-class citizen, Robert? Do you feel that people hate you because you're a Catholic? Well, you ought to, because they do. Don't believe one half of the liberalism you hear, for do you know what they really think we are? Expendable vermin. They don't care how many of us are killed, because we breed fast, and so the numbers go up again. They'd like to see us all dead. The ones with the tattoos and sashes sweating under the weight of a Lambed drum may be the only ones who'll show their hatred but, believe you me, there's a hell of a lot more of them have it hidden in their hearts."

"She's a fanatic," said Robert to Kathy, "a bloody, raving fanatic."

"I'm not," said Theresa, standing up, "but you're blind and self-deluded. Don't ever say that you weren't warned, or that you didn't know." She walked out and Robert and Kathy were left there, stunned by the way in which the little celebration had ended. They sat in silence. Robert topped up their glasses but still they neither drank nor spoke. Against his will, Robert found himself thinking of the first night of a friend's play which he had attended with Kathy only the previous week. A sizeable group of friends, Robert and Kathy included, had gone for drinks afterwards, and the course of the conversation had turned first to politics and then to a particular politician. They had laughed at him. They had ridiculed the way in which he maintained power by playing on the fear of unintelligent people, telling them only what they wanted to hear. They had imitated to perfection his booming, hectoring voice, and laughed as if he were some great harmless buffoon; but then there had been a lull in the conversation and someone had said, "Mind you, there's a lot of truth in some of the things he says." No one had contradicted this. Kathy had looked across at Robert, and Robert had felt afraid.

Kathy now picked up her glass. "Robert," she said slowly, "remember that play we went to see last week?"

"Yes." His voice was harsh, daring her to say what was in both their minds. "What about it?"

Cravenly, she sipped her cheap wine.

"It was very good, wasn't it?"

Late that night, Theresa lay in bed, unable to sleep. It was two years to the day since she had left for Italy with Francis. She could hear the noises of the road: traffic, footsteps, voices. As the night wore on, the sounds became more infrequent and increasingly bizarre. When she heard a drunk man singing "Melancholy Baby," the booming amplification of which suggested that he had borrowed a large plastic traffic cone from adjacent roadworks to serve as an impromptu megaphone, she sighed, picked up her alarm clock and held its luminous dial close to her eyes: 2:25. The voice of the lonely singer tailed off into the darkness. The clock ticked.

She began to think of all the people in Belfast who were drinking or drugging themselves into bearable insensibility that night. People would be hitting other people in the face with broken bottles. People were avowing and making love to people for whom they truly cared nothing; other people were screaming hatred at those whom they really did love. People were destroying things, daubing walls with paint and breaking up telephone boxes; joy-riding stolen cars into stone walls. In hospitals and homes, people were watching others dying, hoping and praying that the inevitable would not happen, while other people were planning murder. People elsewhere were trying to commit suicide, fumbling with change for the gas meter or emptying brown plastic bottles of their pills and tablets, which were bitter and dry in the mouth.

And there are, she thought, there must be, people who think as I do.

Whenever she tried to define for herself her own feelings, she kept coming up again and again with the same images: a wall, a pit, a hole. When Francis died, she felt that she had fallen into a deep, dark pit, with cold smooth sides, out of which it was impossible to climb. She did not deny her desolation, nor believe that she could escape from it either by self-stupefaction or by trying to make others suffer as greatly as she herself had done. She lay in bed, sat, stood or walked and she said nothing and did nothing. She waited, and already this waiting was in progress. She had gone past the stage of the panicked desire to escape to a place where death was not, for she knew now that in all the world no such place existed. She did nothing, for she did not know what she could do that would be of help; there was nothing possible but to sit and feel this pain of her loss and loneliness wander through her soul. She thought with bitterness of people who said that they wanted to live intensely, "in extremis." She did not believe that they understood what they wanted: only a perverse and masochistic mind would think this a desirable state. She did not want to suffer: she wanted to be happy, even though she did not think that this was a laudable desire; but truthfully there were moments, and this was one of them, when she would have changed eternal joy — eternal anything — for mere temporal and finite happiness. She wanted to have Francis back with her. She was saddened by her capacity for forgetfulness: the particular inflections of his voice, the texture of his skin: she had become too used to his absence. She felt a sudden dread of death which was not fear of dying herself, but of being passed over by death, of being left behind, alone. Morbid fantasies concerning her mother flooded her mind. Mammy walking out of the house and having half her head blown away by a stray bullet. Mammy in a shop when a bomb explodes and her body bursting into a scattered jumble of bloody pieces. Mammy being burnt alive in a firebombed restaurant. Mammy —

"No," she said aloud, "no, this is foolish and childish, this fear that she will be killed." But it was the thing which, in all the world she dreaded most. And it was not an illogical fear, for Francis had been killed and Belfast was small: it might well happen again.

At the end, she thought, death must be desirable: Jane Austen heaving her last spiked breaths to say, when asked what she wanted, "Nothing but death"; the wrinkled Sybil, lying withered and motionless save for a bright flickering eye, who said to the inquisitive boys, "I want to die." She could only think that, after he had been so severely tortured (stabbed and beaten and burnt), Francis, too, had felt relief to be at last released into death. And Francis (terrible irony) was the only person in the world whom she loved so much that she would have died for him.

For what the undertaker called "obvious reasons," the lid of the coffin was not removed at any stage of the funeral ceremonies. When they trundled the solid lozenge of pale wood into the hospital's chilly mortuary chapel prior to the removal of the remains, all Theresa's grief was overpowered by anger against the God who could have prevented this but who had permitted it to happen. She would not love such a God and she decided immediately that she would not believe in Him. The undertaker led them in a decade of the Rosary but she did not join in; she stood trembling by the coffin and looked with shock and tenderness at Francis's name engraved upon the little chrome plaque.

Yet to decide not to believe: what did that mean? If God existed, He existed and her refusal to believe could not alter that. The simple withdrawal of her faith (or anyone's, or everyone's) could not destroy God. She had never in her life doubted His existence for a single moment, and she did not doubt it now. This was a problem of love, not faith. God was real: she was quite free to hate Him.

But where did Francis come into this? If there was no God, death was the end and the people who had killed Francis really had destroyed him absolutely, leaving only a body which was too terrible for his own family to see and which would soon be rotting in the grave. This cruel, hated God was her only link with Francis and if she lost God she lost Francis; if she could stop believing in God, she would have to stop believing in her brother.

Each alternative was dreadful: a God with a divine plan, part of which was that Francis should be tortured and shot; or no God and no plan, so that all this was chaos and there could never be any justification or explanation and might really was right. Some people really did have the power to take away the lives of others and no one could ever vindicate or expiate their acts. And she knew that her ineluctable belief did not leave her free to choose her alternative, and although she had resented it deeply only moments before, it offered the only possible shred of comfort.

They concluded the prayers, and as she followed the coffin out to the hearse she resigned herself silently to belief in God and knew that she would have to learn to love Him again, although there was resentment and little understanding in her heart.

As one walks across St. Peter's Square in Rome, the four rows of Doric pillars which form Bernini's Colonnade merge and shift so that they seem to increase then decrease in number and their colour changes from golden-grey to deepest black. There are, however, two small stones in the vast, cobbled square which are the focal points of the sweeping grey arcs and, when one stands upon these stones, all four rows fall into order, so that one sees only a single row of pillars.

Theresa and Francis had found these stones; Francis had stood on one and said simply, "This is what it's like when you begin to believe that God loves you."

She had asked him then how his belief in God affected him, and he had said, "I feel as if I'm being watched all the time, as if a big eye is looking at me and through me for every second of my existence. I see God in everything, but God also sees everything in me. There are eyes everywhere: the sun, moon, stars, every light and every window, but worst of all are the eyes of people. God looks straight out at me through the eye of every human being, asking me to look straight back at Him. But I know that I can't because I'm not good enough, and I can feel the eyes catch on me like hooks. Everywhere I look, I see only eyes, God's eyes, God telling me what He did for me and wanting to know what I'm doing for Him; God looking and looking and wanting me to try to look steadily back."

"That sounds terrible," said Theresa. "I can imagine few things worse."

"Oh, there's something infinitely worse," he exclaimed.

"Which is?"

"Not being looked at at all."

The huge square was thronged. People grouped themselves around the fountains for photographs; tourists scurried in groups behind guides, some of whom brandished a little flag, a closed umbrella or a plastic flower. "Just look at all these people," he said, "a fraction of all those who are now in the Vatican, in Rome, in Italy, in Europe, in all the world; think of all the people who ever were, who are and who will be, and then think that you are just one amongst them all, and that no one in particular is looking at you. No matter how good family and friends are, they can't look at you absolutely in the eye always and forever: it's never perfect, never total. Other people never understand fully and never love fully. Then they die. Oh, I'd much rather be looked at than not!" And so he had known even then the best and most dreadful truth.

When they had finished speaking, she put her arm through his and they walked across the square to the basilica. In spite of the heat and the deep blue sky against which the building loomed, the associations which she instinctively made were of coldness, not warmth, as she remembered the souvenir snowstorm which she had owned as a child. The real basilica evoked the flooded plastic edifice, and its cold, breakable beauty still was there: she felt that the frail cupola, gilded within, could be shivered easily as an eggshell ("for Thine is the KINGDOM, the POWER and the GLORY") just as she had shattered the dome of the snowstorm. Without water, the model basilica had looked pathetically shoddy and small.

Once inside, she tightened her grip on Francis's arm, for as they walked around looking at the beautiful things, at the paintings and statues and magnificent altars and marble floors, she had felt a terrible passion for this God of Whom he had spoken, this God Who looked and looked and Who wanted you to return His gaze; but she was conscious of Him through Francis's words and not through the lapis lazuli, the alabaster or the white Carrara marble. They stopped in front of the Pietà, and she thought, idly, were it not for the distance and the plate glass, how much damage I could so quickly do with a hammer or a hatchet. And then Francis had broken into her thoughts, saying softly, "Were I to break that, I would only be breaking stone. People do not look for God, they look only for bits of metal and stone and glass. They come for art's sake; they don't believe."

"And without belief," she said, "it's just a piece of white stone." He replied that, even with belief, it was nothing more, that it was merely a thing so very beautiful that it obstructed what it ostensibly stood for, which is infinitely more beautiful and which cannot be destroyed.

And that same evening, they had found by chance the little church which houses Bernini's statue of Saint Theresa of Avila in Ecstasy. The air inside was fusty with the smell of burnt wax and stale incense, the church dim and almost empty. Together they stood before the statue, not speaking, until Francis whispered, "It's absolutely beautiful. That's what it is to be lost in the eye which never closes or looks away." She knew what he wanted and she could understand his desire to be in that state, to be like Saint Theresa, stunned into ecstasy by union with God, but she could not fully share that desire and it frightened her. The little white feet were shockingly still among the panicked, ruffled marble folds of the habit. And Francis was looking unflinchingly at the gilded arrow in the hand of the angel. Suddenly, his sister had felt very lonely: she would never feel so lonely again until he died. She turned away, for she could not bear to look at him, and she waited at the back of the church until he was ready to join her.

They left Rome the following day.

Snuggled down in bed with the duvet tucked up around his chin, Robert, with the fascination of a small child, watched Kathy putting on her make-up. She was sitting at the far side of the room before a pier glass which Robert had bought in Smithfield, although she was using mainly her own little hand mirror, which caught sharp flashes of yellow morning light as it streamed through the un-curtained windows to brighten and soften the whole room. She had put Robert's dressing-gown on over her under-wear; the rest of her clothes were draped over a large wicker chair nearby. Not for the first time Robert thought about the possibility of her moving in with him, and how strange and lovely it would be to have her clothes and possessions permanently in his home. The otherness of women fascinated him. "The opposite sex," therein lay the mystery, so different and yet still human! Her clothes were beautiful, piled there in sensuous disorder — her jacket of plum velvet; her soft grey silk blouse, her pale tights, translucent as rose petals. From where he lay he could not, of course, savour the great richness of their smell, which they had acquired from contact with her body. That smell itself was a mystery; a glorious unnamable blend of perfume, cosmetics and something that was Kathy.

If there really were such a thing as magic, he thought, it had something to do with women's bodies.

He watched while Kathy stretched open her deep-set eyes by carefully drawing a mascara brush across each set of eyelashes in turn, an action which he found slightly alarming for the way in which it momentarily lifted the eyelid away from the eyeball. She then smeared a purply-coloured powder on the lids and her eyes remained miraculously wide, their naturally piggy look lost. He watched while she changed the shape of her face by carefully dabbing her cheekbones with an ochre fluid; and while she painted her lips deep red. She kissed a tissue and painted them again, then turned a countenance like a water-colour towards the pier glass to survey the final effect. She saw that he was looking at her looking at herself in his mirror, and without turning round she bounced a smile off the pier glass and across the room to him. The smile revealed a tiny speck of lipstick on her teeth: she carefully wiped it away. She then gathered together all the little bottles and tubes and replaced them in their small corduroy make-up bag, checking in turn that the lid of each was tight.

Robert would have gained a distinctly voyeuristic thrill from watching anyone transform themselves from the sleepy-eyed and tousled person who crept out of bed in the morning into the dressed and groomed creature who normally faced the world: that it was Kathy simply made it more aesthetically pleasing. As a child, it had been a revelation for him to discover that Miss McGuire, the harridan who taught him when he was in Infants, was not born wearing her brown tweed pinafore. She had to undress herself and go to bed every night and she had to dress herself in the morning in layers, just as Robert himself and his family had to do. It took some believing that other people's clothes were like his own and not all of a piece, like the paper clothes which Rosie's cardboard dolls wore, hanging over their printed underwear from the little tabs at their shoulders. It was hard to believe that other people had real lives utterly independent of his own and, more amazing still, that in the humblest and most mundane features these other lives were just like his own. (Oh, the sight of Miss McGuire that Saturday morning, buying a quarter of cinnamon lozenges! And his father's mirth afterwards as he told his mother, "If ye'd seen the eyes of him, near out on two stalks, he thinks she comes up out of the floor to teach him and then goes back down again!") Of all his childhood fancies, this had been the most powerful and the most comprehensive. It was the only one about which he was loath to speak, because it still existed in a residual, but strongly perceptible, form. He liked it when his girlfriends stayed the night with him instead of going back to the empty facades of their family homes to wait for their next cue into his life. By staying and sleeping with him and letting him see them putting on their make-up and their clothes in the morning, they seemed to extend their existence: to re-create themselves. He like that: it helped confirm reality for him.

Kathy was now brushing out her hair. She fastened it up with two combs of tortoiseshell plastic, then moved across the room to a chair by the window and sat in profile to him, looking out into the street.

What was in her mind? Most likely her own sins, he thought. He had never yet met a woman with the guts for atheism; they were all cringing with at least vestigial Christianity at heart. A few nights before that they had inadvertently begun to talk about religion, and when he asked her outright if she believed in God she had said, "No," but with a "No" so reluctant and so diffident that he did not believe it. He had teased and nagged her, "You do, you do, go on, admit it," until at last she lost her temper. "Alright, so what if I do? You can be a right pig, Robert McConville, a right bully."

So what? It put the power of real sin in her hand. Amorality was a bland business, but Kathy was immoral, and spectacularly so. She believed in free choice for right and wrong, and she wilfully, gleefully, chose wrong. It was exciting to dabble with perdition. With a mixture of alarm and sadness, he had listened to the discourse which she poured in his ear one night in bed a short time after he had first known her, a long seamless speech concerning her mother. "So-then-she-said-and-then-I-said . . ." She told him about the scene there had been when her mother found out that she had been sleeping with her boyfriend, information which she had volunteered not because she had to, but because she wanted to annoy. "I hope she's happy now she knows that I'm as bad as she always said I was." It was mainly because of this that he did not believe that she loved him, in spite of her frequent claims to the contrary. He didn't care about being loved but he despised her for lying about it. She had practically admitted to her mother that she did what she did only for the sake of sex and sin, not love. Why, then, would she not admit it to him? As well him as another. Damn, he would make her admit to it, just as he had made her admit to her sneaking religion.

"Kathy," he said, softly, perfidiously, "penny for your thoughts." Would she say something cosmetic and coy — "I was thinking about us"? She shook her head and said nothing.

"Kathy? Come on, tell me." She was silent for another moment before speaking.

"I was thinking about Theresa," she said.

"Oh, *her*," he snorted, disappointed at the inaccuracy of his guess. Now there was one person whom he would not want to see prove their reality in the morning. He would have preferred conclusive evidence that she was merely a figment of his imagination, a bad-tempered, chain-smoking hallucination.

"Yes, Theresa," said Kathy crossly, "and you needn't take that tone when you're talking about her."

"Oh, but Kathy, she's so belligerent, so aggressive. You saw the way she got at me the other day, making a personal attack out of a political discussion."

"You deserved that, Robert, and don't try to tell me

you didn't. She said no more than the truth. If you thought about it at all you'd see that she's right."

"I do think," he said indignantly.

"No, you don't. Oh, come on, Robert, admit it: you pride yourself on being apolitical, away above all that. It doesn't even interest you."

"Well, there's no need for her to be so bloody ardent."

"There's nothing wrong with being ardent, Robert. It's better than being apathetic."

He did not like the direction this exchange was taking; now he would either have to lose face or let it develop into a full-scale row. "She smokes too much," he eventually said lamely. "That really gets on my wick, so it does. Is she on commission from Rothman's, or what?"

"It's nerves," said Kathy.

"Nerves? What has she got to be nervous about?"

"She hardly smoked at all when I first knew her," said Kathy, which was not an answer to the question which he had asked; and saying that she had been thinking of Theresa had not been strict truth, either, for although she had been thinking of her while putting on her make-up, by the time she moved to the window she was thinking of Francis.

Theresa and Francis were twins. They started at Queen's the same year as Kathy and all three were in the same class. They soon developed the custom of meeting each day in the Union for coffee and Mars Bars, while Francis, the most inveterate and most inept doer of crosswords she had ever met, attempted the Simplex puzzle in the *Irish Times*.

"Twelve down. Bubbles on the skin. Eight letters. No idea."

"Blisters. Easy-peas," she crowed. "Gimme another." After his death, Theresa had given her as a keepsake a *Daily Telegraph* book of crosswords in which every single puzzle had been attempted, but not one of which was complete.

From the first she had preferred Francis to Theresa, because she was reserved while he was genuinely shy: he made a much greater effort to be friendly than his sister ever did. They were always together. Sometimes Kathy wondered if Theresa resented slightly her friendship with Francis. She was hurt and surprised when he left college after the Easter vacation in first year, for he had not given even a hint that he was thinking of such a move. When she asked Theresa about it, Theresa said crossly, "Oh, Francis! Don't even start me on that. He said he was leaving Queen's because he couldn't get to grips with it, as lightly as you like, as if it was an evening class in O-level crochet or something. We can't get wit out of him, you might as well talk to the fireplace."

"What will he do now?"

"I shudder to think."

He took a job filling shelves in a city-centre supermarket. Kathy saw him often between his leaving university in the spring and his death that autumn. She used to call into the supermarket and saw him in his brown overall, stacking up jars of instant coffee or putting price labels on tins of condensed soup. She asked him why he did not try to find a more interesting job.

"I like boring work," he said. "It leaves my mind free for higher things. Anyway," he added, "I don't expect to be here for very long," a remark which, with hindsight, she understood even less than she had done at the time. Her friendships with Theresa and Francis became consolidated for their being conducted separately. She was immensely fond of Francis, who had the most tender and lovely smile she had ever seen. When Francis smiled at her she felt important and loved, although in sustained conversation he failed utterly to maintain eye contact; his glance flitting from his shoes to displays of cornflakes to huge yellow posters saying "Low Low Prices." Before they parted, he always dared to look her in the face once more.

He took her out to lunch a few times, to a seedy little café where the sandwiches indecorously turned up their crusts to reveal their fillings; and a solitary, stale pork pie lurked under a perspex dome like the control of a scientific experiment which had gone horribly wrong. "Have a fly's graveyard," he would say, "or a wee cement biscuit, they're nice." Kathy was often lonely, and then she would envy Theresa her gentle, eccentric brother. She had never known two people so close. She wished that she was half of such a loving couple. Maybe if she had had a brother or sister, it might have been like that. It wasn't fair that she was an only child with a mother who didn't care for her and a dead father whom she couldn't even remember, and a fluctuating fund of men, none of whom had ever really cared for her any more than she cared for them. But then Francis died, and she felt guilty for envying Theresa. She knew that the greater the love, the harder it must be now.

She would never forget the first time she saw Theresa back in college after the murder, sitting at a table in the Union, and looking abnormally solitary. She looked incomplete and shockingly different; even her hair and clothes seemed bereaved. Kathy had been unable to approach her then and had gone away and cried and cried. Looking at Theresa alone, she had felt intense pity and fear.

"Think kindly of her, Robert, please. You don't understand her."

"And you do?"

"Not completely, but still better than you do." She came over and sat beside him on the bed. "It's wrong for you to judge her, you mustn't do it." She leaned against him and put her arms around his neck, thinking how very lucky she was to have Robert. At least somebody loved her.

Robert gently removed the plastic combs and ruffled her hair. Bloody women. He would never understand them. He thought Theresa a most unlikely friend for Kathy and wondered what the attraction could be. Probably that of an unplumbed opposite, he guessed. Theresa's strange eyes had their effect seemingly without any willed effort on her part; her gaze was like that of an indolent cobra. She was a right oddity, he thought. In a way she wasn't really like a girl. Never before had he met anyone so angular and androgynous; indeed, never before had he known anyone for so long and so little considered their sex. It had only really come to his attention some two days before their recent argument, when he had been again obliged to give her a lift home from the library. On reaching her street, the door-lock on her side was stuck, so he had leant across to open it, and as he did so, through the thick fog of cigarette smoke which permanently hung around her, he had smelt the faintest whiff of a light, flowery perfume. He felt not the tiniest frisson of sexuality, but a major tremor of shock: for the first time ever, he was conscious of her body. It begged more questions than it answered. He wondered if she was a virgin, but balked at the notion, for he shuddered to imagine what it would be like to kiss her, much less sleep with her. Kissing Theresa, he thought, would be dangerous and painful; it would sting the lips as it did to kiss a poisoned Bible or a religious statue daubed with Belladonna in a Jacobean tragedy. To embrace her would be like driving an iron spike into his chest.

One day when he was small, a wasp had stung him at school. Miss McGuire applied her sovereign remedy for stings, which was malt vinegar painted on with a long-handled sable brush, but he had continued to weep pathetically (the smell of the vinegar was almost as bad as the sting). Miss McGuire then kissed him on the cheek, and he immediately forgot both smell and sting in the shock of discovering that her face was as warm and soft as his own. He still felt that it would be eerie and unnerving to discover by experience that Theresa's body was as warm, soft, mortal and sexual as that of anyone else.

"She never talks about her family," he said.

"No," replied Kathy, "and neither do you." She leant over and kissed him on the lips, which made it physically impossible for him to either answer this retort or to ask any further awkward questions. For the first time that morning, he guessed correctly what was in her mind, but although he knew she wanted to keep him quiet, he could not know the reason why. The ruse worked, however: it provided sufficient distraction to turn his thoughts away from Theresa. He considered her now, together with the other women whom he knew. Theresa, Kathy, Rosie, his mother — what did any of them truly think and feel? And why? None of them were deliberately mysterious and yet they were all a mystery. He wished for understanding for the sake of pure curiosity rather than for the love which he might have had for any of them. There was always an obstruction. He had never felt real unity with any woman; worse, he had never once even reached a consensus by which they agreed to differ. He had drifted away from all the girls he had ever known with no more ultimate intimacy than there had been when they first met. He looked down at the crown of Kathy's head. Did he really want to understand her? No. Did he love her? No, and if he had been mistaken about what was in her mind when she was sitting at the window he was convinced that it was an error of time only. She did delight in what she was doing; he was her sin, he furnished the glamour of her being "bad." So be it. He put his hand under her chin to raise her head and saw, to his puzzlement and utter exasperation, that her eyes were filled with tears.

*   *   *

A black-and-white photograph of her parents' wedding hung over the china cabinet in the parlour, and Theresa's attention was drawn to it again and again. She wondered how her parents — how anyone — went through with a white wedding, for she could never countenance even the possibility of it for herself. She thought that weddings were unspeakably vulgar and almost primitive in their hidebound custom and attention to detail: the white dress, the communal meal of cooked meats and a tall cake, the speeches, dancing and confetti, the crude remarks lip-sticked across the windscreen of a car festooned with toilet paper and old boots. The unhappy happy couple were at least spared the Eastern ignominy of having their entire extended family beating at their bedroom door, demanding proof of lost virginity. As The Preacher said, there is nothing in this world that is new, and white weddings, Theresa thought, like the popular press and much television, are greatly dependent upon unoriginality and repetition for their ultimate success.

It was partly because of this that she found it hard to believe that her mother remembered her wedding day as a real day and not merely in terms of black-and-white photographs, a few dried flowers, some cards and telegrams and a yellowed tulle veil. These objects, like hoiy relics or objects in a museum, alienated Theresa from that to which they pertained, rather than bringing them closer, their frail, folded, dated state stressing for her how very old they were and how far in the past the event had been. It took an effort to remember that her parents' wedding day had been a real day, a day with weather and milk deliveries. She could never fully catch and hold that idea, so that the day remained a series of images. She could make no satisfactory substitute for experience. Her isolation from her parents' marriage made her sad, because it was part of her isolation from her father and it made her very sad to think of his having died before she was old enough to remember him.

Somewhere in the house there was a large manila envelope containing an eclectic array of photographs of her father. There were some fuzzy little snaps stapled into covers of ginger cardboard to form tiny books; and a studio portrait of him when he was twenty, in which he was grinning at the camera with well-fed confidence. There was an oval sepia print of a scruffy little boy with a skew-whiff Eton collar; and a tattered class photograph taken when he was nine, and upon which he had later indicated his own tiny image with a heavily inked "X," completely obliterating the face of the child directly behind him. Theresa's favorite photograph of him was one taken by a street photographer years before her father's marriage. He looked so young and happy, as unaware of death as he was of the eye of the camera. What had happened before and after that instant when, as he passed innocently down the street, a clicking shutter had made of him an eternal image for his unborn daughter? Around him, the city spawned and died. There was a cigarette between his fingers; moments later he would have extinguished it; an hour later smoked another and that evening bought a new packet, moving away from the moment of the photograph and towards his own death. History of some sort had been made that day, for there was never a day so dull that the newspapers had no headlines, but what was for her its only significant event was unrecorded. No paper carried the leader: "Patsy Cassidy Snapped by Street Photographer." She would have given a year of her life to know the day and the hour at which that photograph had been taken. She felt that such knowledge would have given her the power to pluck and save her father from the flux of time.

It was even worse for poor Kathy, she thought. Her mother absolutely refused to talk about her husband, of whom there was not a single extant photograph. Mrs. O'Gorman evidently bore her bereavement through such silence and negation, but it was a source of deep resentment for her daughter. "He might as well never have lived," she said bitterly.

As children, Theresa's father and mother had travelled frequently on the same local train; he and his father going from Belfast to visit a rural grandmother; she and her mother coming up to the city for a day's shopping. On every journey, the train stopped at Lisburn Station and the children saw a large metal advertisement which read "DON'T BE MISLED: CAMP COFFEE IS THE BEST." Independently, they both thought that "misled" was pronounced "mizzled" and wondered what on earth it could possibly mean. Only after their marriage did they discover their shared misunderstanding.

So they met and married, then honeymooned in Clifden, a town which Theresa had never visited and never wanted to visit. She accepted her mother's evocation of Clifden as she accepted Dostoyevsky's Petersburg. Each place was conceived in the memory, language and discourse of others, then took life in her own imagination; the illusory streets and squares and people rose before her. It would be futile to look for these towns, not because they had changed but because in the form in which she saw them they had never truly existed.

This honeymoon Clifden, then, was a dream, and the real nature of her parents' short marriage, the first days of which had been spent there, was also impossible to pin down. Once, only once, had her mother let slip: "It wasn't all roses," and while this did not give the lie to the stories which she told of a kind and happy husband, it showed that the truth was only partial. She wished that her mother would say, "He was sometimes selfish and thoughtless and mean — but only sometimes; I loved him, so it doesn't really matter." While she did not know the whole story, her father remained an affable but unreal stranger. She could not love him.

She could understand her mother's tendency to romanticize the memory of someone simply because they were dead: she did it herself with Francis. As if it had all been so perfect! Never a cross word? At times there had been nothing else. She could make herself forget almost completely the bitter rows they had had when he left university, but that did not mean that they had never happened. When she thought back now, she was still angry, she still thought that she had been right and Francis had been a fool, a stubborn fool.

"A supermarket, Francis? A bloody supermarket?"

"Yes, Theresa, a supermarket. I have to do it. It's what God wants for me now."

"Before He formed you in the womb He knew you, and decreed that you be a filler of shelves, is that what you're trying to tell me? Are you to be a voice crying in the wilderness, '1op off Heinz Beans, this week's special offer'?"

He did not reply to that, but left the room, slamming the door behind him. She never missed a chance to mock and goad him. "I hope you're ambitious, Francis, I hope you aspire to high and noble things, like the bacon counter."

He had once said, "You'll see," but she never did. She still felt that she had failed in not managing to browbeat him back into college and she resented that he had proved his will stronger than hers by not yielding. She still could not see, and believed that she never would see, the virtue of his taking that brainless, pointless, futureless job. She might suspect his motivation, but she could not understand it.

He had had an exaggerated sense of the importance of his own life. He felt so strongly that life was a huge, blank, malleable and significant thing which one had a moral obligation to use fully and properly, that he had eventually frightened himself into doing nothing at all. He dabbled in various things — painting, playing the piano, geology — but never with any great conviction, and his halfhearted plans and projects always came to nothing. Eventually he gave up, and waited for that one big thing, that one act or event which would qualify his

whole life. It was as if by taking the job in the supermarket he was trying to hoard all his energy — trying
to hoard life itself — for that one instant of action, union
and justification. It was similar to the way in which all
the trivialities of an artist's life became subsumed by the
grandeur of his greatest work; but Francis, she thought,
had been no artist. He had, however, been happier at
the supermarket than at Queen's, there was no denying
that. It all seemed so unimportant and foolish now that
the fearfully conserved life was ended. The overwhelm-
ingly significant thing now was her love for him. Even
if she thought that he had been foolish or that he had
shirked life, her love would have to accommodate these
things because they were a part of him.

Where was Francis now? What was Heaven? A place
of total and unqualified love; a place where there was
never, ever the need to say "and yet," "in spite of," or
"nevertheless."

Towards the end of July, a television documentary was
broadcast concerning former terrorists who were now
living in exile in America, unextradited and unrepentant.
Theresa's mother insisted that they watch it, although
Theresa herself had strong misgivings. One man, wearing beach clothes and sitting on a white iron chair by a
sunny terrace, deprecated with a wave of his hand the
luxury in which he now lived. He spoke of the dangers
of his position, and said that he was wanted by both the
British Army and various paramilitary organizations. In
a voice which had acquired a strong American twang, he

spoke of internal organization and communication; cell structures and factions; divisions, battalions and volunteers. Then the interviewer asked him about the actions which had led him to his present exile.

"Did you kill members of the security forces?"

"No comment."

"Did you kill civilians?"

His eyes flitted left and right, looked slyly at the camera, and then looked away again.

"No comment."

"Did you ever take part in any purely sectarian killings?"

He gave a little smile of exasperation.

"No comment."

As Theresa had feared and expected, her mother broke down and cried. "I knew this would happen," she said, and switched off the television, her mother's sobs sounding even more wretched and distressing against the sudden silence which this afforded. Her mother, her sweet, kind, thoughtful mother, who had made big scones, now lay wailing on her chintzy sofa. "I hope they rot in Hell for what they did to Francis, God curse them and their kind."

"They're not all in California ate'n steaks and melons," said Theresa roughly. "The one that did Francis is probably lyin' drunk in a gutter in Sandy Row."

"Does that make it any better? He's alive and doin' what he wants. Francis is lyin' in Milltown."

Theresa also began to cry then. She would never see him again in this world, never never never never never.

She thought that Francis had been beaten; he was an absolute victim. She resented even the longevity of little old ladies with velveteen hats and bile-green knitting, who clung to the railings for support as they toddled up the road to mass and who, merely by staying alive, had in some way bested Francis. Francis was a failure; he had failed even to continue existing. Now they would have to live out the rest of their lives without him.

"Uncle Bobby?"
"Yes?"
"What do you call a dwarf covered in cement?"
"Give up."
"A wee hard man." Tommy crowed with laughter and leapt across the sofa.
"Uncle Bobby?"
"What, Tommy?"
"What's big an' warm an' furry an' would look good on a Protestan'?"
"A fur coat?"
"No, an Alsatian dog."
"Tommy, you stop that," scolded Rosie. "That's not a nice joke, who told you that?"
"Daddy."
"Well, it's not nice. C'm on, feet off the sofa and out with ye; away out to the back scullery an' play with yer worms." Tommy stumped reluctantly out of the room and Rosie wearily drew her hand across her forehead. "God, yer up agin a brick wall tryin' to bring them up right in this day an' age, aren't ye?"

"Yes, indeed," said Robert with sincerity, although he thought that she could have simplified her task considerably by marrying someone other than Tom, Provo or Provo sympathizer or whatever the hell he was, the miserable get. Robert had once seen the butt of a gun sticking out from under a bed in the house, and every time there was an army raid Rosie smashed a few plates or cups and got edgy. Wouldn't it be like the thing for them to lift Tom just when the baby was due? Wouldn't that be a nice picnic? As he thought this, he heard the sinister whine of an army Saracen passing, and against this convenient noise he deliberately asked Rosie, "Do you ever — ah — worry about Tom?" She, with equal deliberation, chose to be evasive, by not associating the sound and the question.

"Worry? Aye, he wants to be there when the baby comes and that worries me alright. He goes to these classes in the Royal and sees films about it and things, but he has no more notion than the cat, Robert." The very thought of seeing a baby being born made Robert feel queasy. How could Tom countenance such a thing? God, but he hated him! He hated him for being so consistently cheerful and irresponsible and happy. He hated him for the way he was always trying to inveigle him, Robert, into talking politics, with his "British war machine" and his "revolutionary struggle" and his "imperialist oppression" and all his other clichés, and his unfailing way of concluding, "Amn't I right, Bobby?" His arguing unnerved Robert as much as it annoyed him, for Tom was persuasive and articulate: in spite of his jargon, he knew what he was talking about. It did not matter whether Tom was right or wrong: what mattered was his blithe and total conviction that he *was* right, which Robert could counter only with ill-informed and badly thought-out arguments, made mainly for the sake of argument. The whole Northern Irish political issue wearied and bored him.

He had met Tom by chance in the city the previous week and had been obliged, with great reluctance, to go for a drink with him, over which Tom had told him a story about an old woman named Eileen who lived in the same street as Rosie and himself.

"Last week," he said, "Eileen, she slipped an' fell at her own front door. There was a foot patrol of Brits goin' past and they stopped to give her a han' an' Eileen of course was effin' an' blindin' an' tryin' to beat them off, the more they were tryin' to help her, seein' as how they were Brits. Well, the leg was bravel an' badly hurt, so she got it all strapped up an' three days later she's sittin' on a chair by her door with the leg propped up before her on a stool. What comes along, but an army lan' rover. It slows down, see, an' one of the Brits sticks his head out of the back an' he calls to her, 'Hello, Eileen, how's your leg?' An' Eileen, Eileen, she calls back, 'Still hingin' from me arse.' "

Tom almost choked with laughter as he came to the punchline of his joke, which Robert did not find particularly amusing. A stream of words drifted into his mind to describe the noises Tom was making: "a coughball of laughter leaped from his throat, dragging after it a rattling chain of phlegm." They were splendid words but they were not Robert's own, and as he watched Tom laughing and coughing he wondered which was worse: the claustrophobia of Belfast or the verbal deficiency which prevented him from adequately describing it.

Rosie sighed and shrugged away the thought of Tom as spectator at her confinement. "I saw your girlfriend the other day," she said, "in Clonard."

"Kathy?" he exclaimed in amazement. "In Clonard?" He did not know, nor care to know, all Kathy's movements when she was away from him, but he could not believe that the chapel of a Redemptorist monastery was one of her haunts.

"No," said Rosie, "not Kathy. I don't know any Kathy. I mean Theresa, the girl you brought here."

"Oh, Theresa," he said. "Were you speaking to her?"

"Yes. She's nice. I feel sorry for her."

"Why?"

"I don't know: there's just something about her."

So the Basilisk went to Clonard, did she? One day when she was outside the library having a fag he would leave a note on her absented desk saying, "Nymph in thy orisons be remembered all my sins." Rosie broke into his thoughts.

"Who's Kathy, then?"

"My girlfriend," he said shortly. "It's through her that I know Theresa."

"Oh." She looked hurt and resentful, but he would still tell her nothing. She was bound to have already a fair idea of his lifestyle, but the details would shock her.

To suspect was one thing, but to know was quite another, and he was afraid that he would alienate her in exactly the same way in which he had alienated his mother. It would have been little comfort to her to say: "Rosie, I couldn't tell you the things even if I really wanted to." There were things of which he was too ashamed. He could never tell her about what he had done on the night of their mother's death.

On the evening when her remains were brought from the house to the chapel he had, immediately on returning from the short service, gone up to where she had been laid out. He was taken aback by the ravished air of the little room. A small oleograph of the Sacred Heart had been tilted askew on the wall by the press of mourners. A few velvety petals had dropped from the little vase of roses on the dressing-table, the mirror of which was sheeted. On top of the chest of drawers were long pennons of paper which were printed with crucifixes and all stuck with beaded rods of creamy wax. The pennons were crumpled and torn as a result of having been removed from the candlesticks in great haste by the undertakers. Then he saw the bed with its quilt depressed and slightly dragged to one side, as if his mother had been merely sleeping there for half an hour in the afternoon, rather than lying in her coffin. But you could rumple beds with something other than sleeping or death, and that very night he brought a girl back to his flat and frightened her with passion.

She in turn startled him afterwards by saying suddenly, "I spy with my little eye something beginning with B.T."

"What?"

"Black tie. Who's dead?" she said playfully.

"My mother."

He felt her body stiffen, and her voice changed.

"When?"

"Last year. I bought the tie for her funeral; it must have fallen out of the wardrobe."

"Oh," she said. There was a pause, then he felt her body relax again. "God," she chuckled, "you had me worried there for a minute."

He regretted his cowardly lie, even though the girl would probably have fled the place had he told her the truth. She never knew that she was turfed out early the following morning so that he could prepare for the funeral. Rosie would think he was an utter monster if she knew, and perhaps he was. If he had slept with a girl and was then told that her father had died the previous day he would have been shocked, so he felt that the shock of others was justifiable. He tried to remember the girl's name, and felt with a pang of regret that his grief had taught him nothing. He realized that Rosie was watching him beadily, and he fidgeted uncomfortably in his chair.

"The less you know about me the better, Rosie," he said.

"Better for you or for me?"

"For both of us. I'd best be off." He stood up.

"Robert, sometimes I wonder why you come here at

all," she said, her voice hardening with uncharacteristic anger. "D'ye like to remind yerself how far ye've come? Cos I'll tell you something — it might not be just as far as ye think."

Little Tommy held to his eyes an oblong of red plastic, thrice dimpled, in which had nestled some of Mr. Kipling's Exceedingly Good Jam Tarts. He saw the world in the round; rosy-pink when the light was strong and changing deeper to red as the light dimmed; and he saw it roughly because of the way in which the plastic was stippled. The view he obtained of his home city was thus narrow, inaccurate and highly coloured: defensible in a five-year-old peering through a piece of cake-box packaging, but not in the older citizens who shared his vision. The violence and political struggles had effected less change than was generally acknowledged: it had not altered Belfast's perception of itself. It remained an introverted city, narcissistic, nostalgic and profoundly un-European (this latter in spite of one's now being able to purchase there croissants in tins).

Robert worked hard that summer, primarily in the fine arts department of the Central Library. He frequently raised his eyes to the little artist's pallets which formed part of the stucco ornamentation around the ogee'd skylight, and inwardly he groaned. He felt that he deserved something better than the boredom of summer in Belfast, and the dull, uncreative work on which he was engaged. He had vaguely expected a more exciting, a more fulfilling life, and only in instances did he realize that it had not materialized and that it probably never would. In lucid flashes, he feared that this tedious summer was a microcosm of his whole future life: lonely, frustrating, dull, dragged out in a lunatic, self-destructive city. He could not have defined the life he wanted; could not have named another person whose art or scope he desired. Perhaps every life was unsatisfactory; perhaps the feeling which predominantly united humanity was not loneliness or love, but a deep sense of failure. He knew no one whose life seemed a fair compensation for the horror of having to die.

The only new person whom he had met that summer was the unlikable Theresa, whose newness and surliness gave her at least a certain novelty value. She also frequented the fine arts department, and was there almost as often as Robert, her desk piled with books and papers, journals, magazines and literary reviews. Her labours seemed even more aimless and unsatisfactory than Robert's, lost in a welter of paper, reading erratically or scribbling in a large red notebook. At worst she was killing time in the library, putting in a summer which had to be got through in some way; at best she was trying to make sense of things through what she read and wrote, but it gave her little comfort. Her own definitions were unsatisfactory; but what she read frequently confirmed her fear that loneliness was inescapable.

"Death is like a fisher who catches fish in his net and leaves them in the water for a little while; the fish is still swimming but the net is around him and the fisher will draw him up — when he thinks fit." She wondered if people in general shared her iceberg mentality: was it common to feel that only a tiny facet of one's self was exposed and communicable to others, with the rest locked in ice, vast, submerged and impossible? She caught Robert's glance as it passed between his desk and the stucco, and she surprised him wih a tiny, timid smile.

Possibly other people were like this unconsciously, and did not realize how little they were known and understood by those around them, nor how little they knew or understood of themselves. Her daily life was very mundane that summer. She idled in the library and in bookshops, frequently had lunch with Kathy and went to occasional films, plays and art exhibitions. She went to mass often and lived quietly, peaceably, with her mother, who did not realize just how few friends her daughter had. Except for Rosie, who thought that there was something sad about her, no one realized that practically her every thought was an unhappy one, and that she was being quietly ground down by constant nagging, absolute distress. She complained frequently of being tired, exhausted even: no one could understand why. She wondered if sometime she would scream aloud what often screamed in her mind: "No! Leave me to have my own life!" If only he had been a husband or a lover, anything but a brother. His death had pitched her into love as much as grief; rather, it let her see how deeply and hopelessly she had been steeped in love, in utter passion for him since the day of their birth. But he was her brother and now he was dead, so that this love was exclusively of the family; worse, of the grave. She swung from feelings of betrayal and revulsion at the idea of similarly loving anyone else to desperate loneliness from the knowledge that she could not do so. She thought that love should not make her feel so trapped, but it did, and she felt it beyond her power to change this.

Her mother told her that she was wasting her summer.

"You ought to take a holiday before you go back to college."

Theresa shrugged indifferently.

"Go abroad," her mother said.

"No."

While in Italy with Francis, she had had a bar of sandalwood soap, and in the course of the journey the atmosphere of that summer had seeped into the soap, so that forever afterwards the smell of sandalwood made her immensely sad, evoking the hot, crowded trains, with their little pull-down seats in the corridors; fusty churches; great art; bitter coffee; and the shabby hotels and inns where they had put up. In Trieste, they found lodgings from a tourist office, where the girl was so anxious that they did not confuse the two inns of the particular street to which she was sending them ("The other one is not at *all* nice") that they became convinced it was a brothel; a conviction strengthened when they saw how very seedy was the establishment to which they had been carefully directed. While the owner was copying their names from their passports for registration, Francis whispered to Theresa: "You wouldn't see that in Ireland," and nodded towards two framed pictures hanging on the wall only inches apart; one a gaudy print of the Madonna and Child, the other a highly erotic etching of a female nude.

Trieste was a forlorn post whose glory had crumbled away when an empire fell and left it sitting bleak, uneasy on a frontier. Theresa and Francis soon wondered why they had gone there, for there was little to see or do, and that little obscured by a sea mist which hung persistently over the bay for the few days they were there. They stood down by the harbour, where dry grass sprouted between broken cobblestones and diseased, scabby pigeons picked around their feet. Francis claimed that he could see things in spite of the fog. He pointed out the Miramare, the Faro and distant ships, but Theresa could see nothing.

"It's your poor wee turney eye," he teased her, "that's what's wrong. Mustn't Mammy have been fierce disappointed when you were born and she saw the eye rollin' in your head? I can see her sittin' up in bed in the maternity ward with the baby in her arms, shakin' it and tiltin' it to try to get the eye to roll into position, like one of those games you used to get in the lid of a tube of Malteasers at Christmas, where you had to roll three ball-bearings into three wee dimples."

"Meanie," said Theresa. "I'll have you know that some people find my eye very attractive."

From Trieste they went to Venice, and only a few hours after their arrival she fell ill with cramps. She told Francis to go out and leave her to suffer alone in peace, and promised that she would meet him by the door of St. Mark's Basilica three hours later. When the time came,

she felt weak but sufficiently well to walk the short distance from the pensione to St. Mark's Square, which she
had not yet seen.

A drawing-room indeed; elegant, timeless, beautiful.
Here was where the doges had thrown rings of flowers
into the water to marry the city to the sea. Real ladies
in heavy, trailing silk dresses had moved beneath the
loggia, and all seemed fused to a timeless perfection, the
past and the present, the fictional and the religious. It
was evening, and the sun fell slantingly against the walls
of the Palace; the sky was turbid and promised thunder.
Some light rain had already fallen, and the stones of the
square were bright and wet. There were many people
there, mostly tourists, all strangers; and then suddenly
she had seen Francis's face materialize out of the crowd,
as familiar to her as her own foot or finger. This was
what she had been seeking, and the faces of all those
other people were masks, dross, distortions, faces which
were wrong: suddenly the only right and real face in
Venice had appeared.

As she watched him move across the damp marble
towards her, she felt a sweep of love which was the sole
complement to the loneliness she would feel before the
statue in Rome, and this loneliness and love would be
fused together in the black moment of grief when she
learnt that he was dead.

In Venice, a man with an umbrella hat had tried to
sell them handfuls of birdseed, which they refused, and
they refused more vehemently the photographer who
attempted to hand to them a toy gondola on which was

perched a miserable-looking little monkey in a blue-and-white-striped knitted suit, with a small hole in the seat of the trousers out of which hung a long, long tail. Francis had impressed her with his knowledge of the history, art and architecture of the city, and with the sensitivity of his response to the beauty around him.

"You're wasting your life, Francis," she said. "Please, why don't you think again? Change jobs, or go back to college."

He frowned. "It's too late."

"Nonsense, it's never too late, how could you..."

"I mean for college. It's too late for me to apply for re-entry for this autumn."

"Next year, then."

"I don't think so. I don't know, Theresa. I'm sure of nothing. Look, leave it and I'll see in the winter, when I'm home and settled, alright?"

"Alright, then."

But before the autumn ended, he was dead.

The coda to that summer was a day spent in Lugano when they were on their way home, and by the side of the lake they saw a small boy with golden-tanned skin and a navy sailor-suit who was tossing little pebbles to break and break again the lake's still surface. He was quite unaware that he was being watched, and Theresa and Francis looked at him for a long time before Theresa spoke.

"If we had been here a hundred years ago, we might well have seen such a child."

Francis continued to look at him and did not answer her for quite some time, then said, "Yes. When you think of that and continue to look at him he ceases to be a particular small boy and becomes the eternal small boy. We're all like that. Everything we suffer has been suffered before, everything that gives us joy has been enjoyed before. Nothing is new: but that doesn't make it any easier to suffer."

"And joy?"

He smiled. "It doesn't diminish joy."

And the summer's final image was a little Lugano fountain, the basin of which had been painted sky blue. People had dropped coins into the water for wishes and good luck, and the blue paint was marked with brown or green rings where the coins had lain and corroded. A stream of bright, fresh water spurted to the sky through a thin bronze pipe, and as it tumbled down to the painted bowl it caught and warped the sunlight. They dipped their hands in the cold water and accidentally their fingers touched. Now, when she tried to visualize the distant Heaven where Francis was, her imagination balked and she could think only: perhaps a well of light; perhaps a stream of bright water ascending to the sun, spurting upwards and away from a small, blue, painted, tainted bowl.

Night had fallen. Robert sat by his desk and stared obliquely at the window, behind which a perfect image of his room was suspended in the dark air. He arose and walked to another chair so that he, too, was now reflected and was thus substantially within and insubstantially without. Glumly, he stared at his dark doppelgänger, which stared back as it floated above the street in its intangible apartment. Could this room and this person, who looked so solid and so real, actually be a mere reflection, nothing more than a trick of glass, air and light? Yes, it was just that, and he found the realization liberating. The reflection looked like him but it was not him: this is me, he thought, refined to perfection. A shadow upon glass could not feel worried or lonely. It could not have a sister or a girlfriend or a dull book to compile. Its body could not feel pain. I should write to the papers, he thought, and say political initiative be damned! The solution to the Irish crisis is for everyone to live by night, to put strong lights in their rooms and draw back the curtains and so make a whole new population identical to the one here now in all things but reality. Let these dark illusions live our lives for us: they will do it much better than we can. For how can a reflection hate? Or be bigoted? Or kill? How could it ever know the futility of suffering? He gave a little laugh which his dark double mirrored. He wished that he could stop being himself and become that double so that he could be dissolved into nothingness when the morning came.

He turned from the window and looked back into his own room. It made him feel ill. He wondered why he accumulated so assiduously this arty clutter of books and prints and rugs and trinkets; such having and hoarding struck him as rather pathetic. Often he felt genuinely queasy just to think of the vast glut of personal possessions in the world. On his way to the library in the mornings, he tried not to imagine all the things which people around him in the streets had recently used; tried to keep at bay a nightmare vision of countless tea-bags and crusts and toothbrushes and combs and bus tickets and socks. Too much reality was hard to bear. He liked to see the private lives of girls in the morning, but one at a time, please! What fascinated him singly revolted him en masse, and the most haunting image he retained from reading about the Holocaust was that of the liberating Allied troops finding the vast mounds of clothing which had been taken from the prisoners on their arrival, including the swallow-tail coats and expensive evening dresses of some wealthy Viennese Jews arrested at a gala evening.

He had gone back to Rosie that afternoon to end a week of festering ill-feeling, although he had gone not knowing whether it was to demand an apology or to make one. In the event, neither happened. Rosie received him kindly and behaved as if nothing had happened, until he brought the subject into the open.

"Oh, let's forget it," she said. "It's not important, we all lose the rag now and then, what does it matter?"

She made tea for him, and their subsequent conversation was overlaid by bangs and thumps from the upper storey, which he presumed, correctly, to be caused by Tom. After a time the banging stopped, they heard heavy feet on the stairs, and then the feckless beast stuck his head around the living-room door, giving a surprised grin when he saw Robert.

"What about ye, Bobby, I never knew ye were in. Nobody tells me nathin' around here."

He had been assembling a cot for the new baby and had come down to tell Rosie that the job was complete. With characteristic bonhomie, he insisted that Robert come up to see his handiwork, and so they all trudged up the narrow stairs to a tiny back room, where little Tommy was waiting with the new cot.

"There," said Tom, picking up a small, thin mattress printed all over with pandas. "Bung in this yoke an' Bob's yer uncle."

"Bob is my uncle," chirruped Tommy and they all laughed, except Rosie, who only smiled and tenderly stroked the veneered chipboard. Watching their innocent delight, Robert realized that he saw before him a thing rare in modern times: familia intacta. They had problems and would have many more; in so many ways he found them pathetic, contemptible, even, but there they were, undeniably real, united and happy. He thought of the other families he knew, broken or decimated, and re-membered reading somewhere that the family was the only social unit which could survive beyond the grave. Hamlet, I am thy father's spirit. Two bright Cumberland eyes had peeped from a bonnet, their owner insisting, "Nay, Master, we are seven." Tom and Rosie beamed shyly at each other and Robert's throat tightened. He hated himself for being moved by scenes of such maudlin sentimentality; it was worse than crying at *The Sound of Music*. He could never see himself in the role of family man, but here, in this tiny bedroom, he now felt the lonely pangs of a monk who, on Saturday afternoons, watches at play the children of men and women who have come to the monastery for blessings, honey and fortified wines, and knows that he will never have a family of his own.

What did it matter that all Rosie's taste was in her mouth? He looked up from his chair to the print of a Van Gogh self-portrait which he had acquired a short time before one of Rosie's rare visits to his flat.

"Who's that?"

"Van Gogh. It's a copy of a painting he did of himself. Do you like it?"

"He could have smiled."

He had tried then and he tried now to imagine Vincent beaming down from his frame, jolly and avuncular, but at both attempts he failed. Now he, Robert, had at least the grace to smile.

Rising from his chair, he crossed to the window. For a moment he again looked out into the phantom room and stared deep into the eyes of his dark fetch until he could bear it no longer. Abruptly, he let the blind drop.

Theresa looked at her hand where it lay on the pillow by her face, and with the heightened perception of extreme pain noted the details of her fingers: the tiny vertical ridges along the nails, the arrangement of the lines in the skin across her knuckles; the conspicuous absence of half-moons. She was relieved that she had not risked going to the library that morning to startle the other readers by falling over her desk with a low and horrible moan. She had realized what was happening at breakfast-time, and now, two hours later, the pain had arrived, intense as a knife wound. For two days she had felt like a piece of rotting fruit, and now she cried and moaned and bit the pillow and swore and cursed everything with the comprehensive rage of someone in extreme, inescapable pain. The most spectacularly obvious feature of pain was its unfairness, descending like a dark bird of prey at that arbitrary moment to her frail and mortal body, rather than to the equally frail and mortal body of someone else. Why me? Why not? She cursed the nurse who, years before, had answered her wail, "Is there anything can cure this?" by giving her two aspirins, patting her head and saying, "It'll be better when you're married, dear." Every so often, she screamed aloud from utter despair that she could not escape from this weak, hateful body, from anger that this piece of agonising rubbish was the only thing which kept her from death. She deeply resented the extent to which she *was* this body. She kept turning to look at the clock — the passage of time was her only hope. Twenty minutes, half an hour, three-quarters, and the agony had ebbed away, leaving her weak and whimpering, like a half-drowned person washed up upon a beach; by the time an hour had passed, she had already forgotten how awful it was.

It was always the same. When she was in the depths of pain, across the fragments of resentment and self-pity would flash the amazed thought: some people live like this. Some people's lives centred around intense and constant pain every single day, so that they could do nothing but suffer and be, their whole existence telescoped into the eye, womb, bowel or leg in which the pain lived, like a savage and belligerent animal. But only when in pain herself could she empathize with this, for immediately afterwards, although her mind of course remembered, her body instantly forgot. By that afternoon, she would be ashamed of the fuss which she had made over a little cramp, and although while in pain she would have done anything, literally anything, to escape, when it was over she knew that she would do nothing to prevent its inevitable recurrence. This was how some people lived, and this was how Francis had died. She felt that she needed to endure occasionally the communion of extreme agony which was beyond the power of memory, much less imagination. She held pain in a certain awe.

It was hard, however, to accept the power of the body over the mind: one cannot simultaneously read Yeats and cry into a pillow, and so in defiance that afternoon, although still feeling weak and tired, she bundled herself up and went down to the library. Her presence was her only triumph for, try as she might, she could not concentrate. She sighed, fingered the pages of a review, popped a Polo mint into her mouth and stared idly at the book shelves. Looking at the spines of erudition intimated to her all the knowledge that lay before her. She knew a little about literature: how insignificant her knowledge of music and art; how non-existent her knowledge of anything scientific! $E-mc^2$ and everything was relative, but what did it mean? Perhaps most demoralizing of all was her ignorance of her own pitiful body, which had made her suffer so much that morning. Where, she wondered, are my kidneys? How big is an ovary? What shape is a pancreas? She tried to imagine her lungs and saw them as a bigger version of the sheep's lungs which she had once seen being fed to a dog and which had been like two red-and-white mottled sponges, but her own lungs would be lightly lacquered over with a fine ginger tar. Then she saw mortality coming, saw a surgeon peel back her skin, lift away the frail cage of her ribs to reveal her lungs, still warm and moist and mottled. They rose and fell, rose and fell, while the surgeon gently stroked the surface with a long, white sterile forefinger.

Even they don't know it all, she thought defiantly. The body still kept its secrets and always would. They had not yet fully unravelled the mysteries of the long, dark ribbons of chromosomes coiled and replicating at the heart of every cell. They had put men on the moon, but Theresa's body remained an undiscovered country.

Robert came into the library at that moment, and saw Theresa before she saw him. He thought that she looked even worse than usual. Glancing up, she saw him and thought, "Please don't come over." He walked straight across to her desk.

"Hello," he said. "I have a message for you from Kathy. She wants you to go over to her house this evening, she wants to talk to you about something."

"You don't know what it is?"

"No. She said go any time after five and she'll give you tea."

Theresa was silent. She was very tired, and had foreseen an evening of coffee, toast, cigarettes, vacuous television and then sleep, sleep and more sleep. She didn't want to trudge over to Harberton Park and risk being insulted by that horrible woman again.

"She said that if you can't go you're to phone her and she'll arrange to see you tomorrow."

"Sounds important."

"Quite."

Theresa sighed deeply. "Very well then. I'll go. You've no idea...?"

"No, none."

"Oh. Well, thanks for the message, anyway."

Theresa knocked timidly at the door, afraid that she would be again surrounded by a trio of yapping, snapping dogs, but there was silence until she heard Kathy's heels clatter across the parquet floor of the hall.

"Come in."

Her eyes were red, and when Theresa stepped into the house the two girls saw themselves reflected, side by side, in a vast oval mirror. They both looked pale and ill.

"You're safe this time," said Kathy, in a very stilted voice. "I have the three dogs locked in the garage, and the bitch is out, and I know that's a terrible thing to say about your own mother, but wait till you hear what I have to tell you. Food first."

She led the way to the kitchen, where she put the finishing touches to two plates of chicken salad, put coffee in the filter for later and cut two large slices of gateau. They carried the food through to the dining-room on a tray, and ate sitting on fat, red velvet chairs with cabriole legs. Neither of them ate much, pushing pieces of chicken and lettuce aimlessly around their plates with large silver forks. Theresa noted that, although Kathy was obviously deeply distressed, in her own home she still fell into the role of good hostess, and had not neglected napkin rings or a posy of flowers in the centre of the table, the colours of which matched the designs on the china and the table linen. It seemed such a ridiculous facade when she was obviously so upset, and eventually Theresa said, "Look, give me that. Make the coffee, forget about the cake and tell me everything."

"It's about my father," said Kathy. "You know I told you that he's dead."

"Yes," said Theresa.

"Well, he's not." She was struggling to keep her voice steady. "He's alive. He lives in London." From her pocket she drew a crumpled envelope. "This letter arrived this morning. He wrote to say that he didn't know how much I knew about him, but that he was sorry for all the time lost. He wants to see me. He sent me a cheque so that I can go over to London to see him. Can you imagine it, Theresa? Can you imagine it? I thought that he was dead!"

"Some people might be very happy to receive such a letter."

"Happy? My father deserts my mother and myself when I'm a baby; she divorces him and tells me lies, tells me he's dead, and then he waits over twenty years before he cares enough to ask if I'm living or dead. That's supposed to make me happy?" said Kathy angrily.

Theresa sat quiet, trying to imagine how she would feel if the dead father of the street photograph, with his smile and cigarette, were to suddenly write to her and suggest that they meet. That the neverness of death could be so suddenly reversed . . . It was little wonder that Kathy was distressed.

"He's married again now," said Kathy slowly. "And he has two little girls. Their names are Cissie and Lizzie. Isn't that nice? Cissie is ten and Lizzie is twelve. I'm sure they're sweet, Theresa, just think, two little girls. I have two little sisters . . . I . . . Theresa . . . I . . . I can't . . ."

She broke down and cried and cried and cried. Theresa fetched a box of paper handkerchiefs and let her cry her fill. When she was calmer and wiping her eyes with her fists, Theresa said cautiously, "May I ask you something, Kathy?"

"What?"

"Does Robert know about this?"

Kathy gave a huge sigh. "No."

"Why not?"

She took a deep breath and replied very slowly.

"I wanted to tell him. That was one of my first reactions. Tell someone. Tell Robert. So I phoned him and said that I wanted to meet him for lunch and he agreed.

So we met. Theresa, I could not tell him. I wanted to, I tried to, but it would not come. I sat there waiting and waiting and said to myself, now, now, tell him now, but I couldn't do it. I opened my mouth and either I said something else or closed my mouth again without having said anything. Eventually he said that he was going back to the library, so I asked him to give you a message if he saw you: to ask you to come here this evening."

"I see."

"My mother's away for a couple of days: that'll be a nice showdown when she comes back. I'll never forgive her for this. I'll never forgive either of them." She paused for a moment, then said, "But Robert . . . It worries me so much that I couldn't tell Robert, for I felt at first that it put a big gap between us, and then I saw that this gap had always been there, and that this just made me admit to it. Lately I haven't known what to make of things. Sometimes I feel in my heart — this sounds terrible, but it's the truth — sometimes I felt that he really despised me because I loved him so much. I felt that he was using me. And sometimes I even wondered if I loved him because he was there — because there was no one else, so perhaps I was using him too . . . God, Theresa, it's such a muddle. I hardly know who I am anymore, nor where to go nor what to do."

"Sleep on it," said Theresa. "Wait for a few days before you decide anything. Things like this need time to settle."

"Yes. Yes, I suppose so. Thank you for listening to all this, Theresa. You have no idea what this means. You're the only one, you know," said Kathy, and for the first time that evening her voice was firm and steady. "You're the only real friend I have: you're the only person that I really and truly love."

Robert and Kathy sat in the Bonne Bouche Café, taking Earl Grey tea and little buns. Kathy looked prettier than Robert had ever before seen her, with her long, dark, silky hair piled artlessly on top of her head, little coils and tresses escaping from their fetters at the back of the neck. He could not help but wonder what went on in the mind beneath all that hair. For over a week now she had been acting oddly. She wouldn't sleep with him and when he was in any way affectionate towards her, it seemed to make her either sad or annoyed. There was something rather cold in her recent conduct, and when he had asked one night what was wrong she had replied, "Nothing," so vehemently that he had been afraid to ask again. And now here she was, saying that she was leaving Belfast within two days.

"To go where?" he asked.

"London."

"Oh." He paused for a moment, then she saw panic and horror in his face as he jumped to the wrong conclusion. She went very red and looked away.

"Don't be so horrible and suspicious, Robert, it's only for a holiday," she muttered crossly.

"Really?"

"Yes, really," she snapped.

"Oh. This is all very sudden, isn't it?"

"I suppose so, but what does that matter? I'm bored

with Belfast and college'll be starting up again soon enough. I just felt that I needed a break before that."

"Are you going alone?"

"Yes, yes, of course. With whom did you imagine I might be going?"

"How would I know who you might go off with?" he said harshly. He realized that he was staring angrily across the room and intimidating a rather elderly waitress, so he lowered his eyes and tried to speak calmly.

"What will you do over there?"

She poured out more tea. "Go to the theatre, go to the art galleries, go out to Kew to see the pagoda, watch the changing of the guard: the usual things one does when in London, I suppose. It's only for a week, you know."

"I hope you enjoy it," he said, with all the sarcasm he could muster.

"Yes, so do I," she said lightly, then she abruptly put down her teacup. "Do you want to talk to me about something, Robert?" she asked angrily. "Do you want to have one of those heavy what's-gone-wrong-with-our-relationship discussions?"

"Do you?"

"No." He glanced at her little hand, which was resting on the table-cloth: she noticed this and immediately withdrew it.

"You will wait for me, won't you, Robert?" she taunted him. "You will be good while I'm away?"

Robert stood up, hurt and confused. "That," he said, "I cannot promise. Enjoy yourself without me."

"I will," she replied, and she had to call it across the café, for he was already at the door.

Robert had found Belfast dull and tedious even with the palliative of Kathy's company. Without it, he found his loneliness and boredom verging on the unbearable. He had many other friends and he now made an effort to see and entertain them, but he missed Kathy inordinately. He wondered and worried about her going off like that so suddenly, and he regretted deeply the row in the café. With anyone else, the bed would not have been cold before he was at least attempting to charm a replacement into it, and he was surprised to find that he now could not bring himself to do this. He missed her in every possible way, and every so often he hated himself for missing her, and told himself that she wasn't worth it.

In his flat he found a silk scarf which bore her smell, and a copy of Thomas Mann's *The Magic Mountain*, which bore her bookplate. He tied the former around the bar at the foot of the bed and attempted to read the latter, remembering Kathy's enthusiasm for it, but found it impenetrable. He forced himself to plough through the novel, but retained little, save perhaps the image of the girl with the handkerchief and orange perfume, and the passage concerning X-rays as a means of seeing into the diseased, mortal, dying body of a woman, which he found both disturbing and oddly titillating. On the fourth evening after Kathy's departure, he had just wearily cast the book aside, wondering if Kathy had been lying when she said that she enjoyed it, and uncorked a bottle of cheap wine to blur his misery when the doorbell rang. His astonishment when he opened the door and found Theresa standing there was total.

"Good evening."

"Hello." He stared at her blankly.

"May I come in, please? It's rather cold out on the step."

"Of course." He opened the door wider and she passed through into his room, a strong smell of cigarettes trailing in her wake.

"I see you're reading *The Magic Mountain*."

"Yes."

"Wonderful, isn't it?"

Robert made a non-committal noise as reply. "Why have you come?" he asked bluntly.

"Social call," she said with a sweet smile, as she removed her jacket. "Alright?"

"Yes. Fine." He went into the kitchen and brought out another wine glass.

"May I put on some music?"

"Yes."

Soft clicks from the stereo were succeeded by strains of Wagner. Her strange behaviour in his own home made Robert feel uneasy. He offered her a glass of wine, which she accepted but left sitting untasted in front of her for a long time, and she did not speak. Slowly the truth dawned on him: she was carefully, lucidly and extremely drunk, and just as he realized this she downed the glass of wine in a single gulp and began to speak.

"Come the revolution, Robert, what do you think will happen? Will the weak merely overthrow the powerful? The poor overthrow the rich? Or is it possible that at last the ugly will overthrow the beautiful? The uncultured overthrow the cultured? More wine. Do you ever think about that, Robert?"

"No," he said, reluctantly refilling her glass.

"Well, you ought to, because we need to know whose side we'll be on when it happens, oppressors or oppressed. Whose side are we on now? We need to know that first."

"I see," he said, seeing nothing.

She was quiet for a few moments, then said, "Wonderful music." They listened to it for a few moments, then she added, "He was Hitler's favourite composer, you know. The Israeli Philharmonic still refuses to perform his works." Wagner soared on. "Today, Robert, all art aspires to the condition of Muzak. It is the noise against which real life happens." She spoke very slowly and carefully. "This is the century which has seen art become more debased than at any other time. Because there was a war, Robert, with concentration camps where a string quartet played Mozart while a man who liked good music had a line of people pass before him and he decided which of those people should live and which should die. Things happened in those camps, Robert, and in that war, which were so terrible that art could not cope with them, and just as all the paintings and music and books in the world were unable to prevent those things happening, afterwards the artists found that they could not produce books or paintings or music which could express that horror. But no one admitted this. The artists would not openly admit defeat. They were like priests who stop believing in God but who keep on going through the motions of religion rather than trying to face or find an alternative. And so more books and paintings and music have been produced since that time than ever before. Because people need something pretty to hang on the walls of their living-rooms. They need agreeable noises to flood their ears. They need stories to distract them from the passage of time. They need art, Robert, to clutter their minds, because if they did not have art they would be forced to look into the silence and emptiness of their own hearts. And the artists conspire with them in this. This is the art we need now, Robert."

She got up, lifted the needle from the record and the room was at once filled with silence.

Robert put his head in his hands, unable to believe what he was hearing. He cursed his luck at being invaded by a drunken female philosopher.

"Doesn't this bother you, Robert? You're supposed to be a writer."

The "supposed" found its target. "No, it doesn't bother me," he replied grumpily. "You're trying to say that art is, or should be, dependent upon politics, and I don't believe that. You're trying to give art a moral function."

"That's what it had long ago."

"Well, not any more."

"That's what I'm trying to tell you!" she cried. She drank her wine and filled her glass again. " 'Truth is beauty, beauty truth.' You still believe that, Robert?" He did not reply. "What does art do?"

He would not reply.

"What does art do?" she yelled.

He shrugged, not wanting to get embroiled in this pointless row. "It makes you more alive," he said eventually.

"You try telling that, Robert," she said, "to all the people in this world who are suffering and dying."

As she spoke, he remembered the moment of his mother's burial, when he had suddenly felt that he was the person in the coffin who was being lowered out of life. He was conscious of familiar faces growing smaller around a rectangle of light: then silence and darkness. An overwhelming sense of the absolute futility of his life and labours swept over him, and he heard Rosie say in a small, sad voice, "It makes ye wonder what it's all about."

"Christ Almighty, Theresa!" he exploded. "Leave me be!" He gazed at her with revulsion as she cowered in a huge, white, wicker chair: sullen, skinny, pale, cross-eyed, drunk, grotesque. It was a very long time before she spoke again.

"Why don't you write about the troubles here, Robert?"

"I don't want to."

"Why not?"

"They don't interest me. I don't understand them."

"God curse your indifference. What does understanding matter? Nobody understands. Some people say that they can see both sides, but they can't. You can only ever see one side, the side you happen to be on. But you haven't the guts for that, Robert: you haven't the guts to be partial, ye spineless liberal."

"Don't you think it's time you were going?" he said coldly, picking up her jacket.

"No."

"It's very late."

"I haven't said all I came to say."

He tossed her jacket onto a chair. "Say it, then, and go."

"Kathy has gone to London to see her father and sisters." She saw his face change. "I thought that might interest you."

"Her father's dead."

"So you think. And so she thought. But he's not. He's alive and well and living in London. And he's married, with two little daughters. Sisters for Kathy. So you see, Robert, you've lost her."

"What do you mean? She's coming back."

"But not the same as she was when she went away. She's found her family, Robert. You know she won't be the same again."

And Robert understood perfectly.

Theresa began to cry. Had this happened only moments before, he would have sworn at her and possibly put her out into the street. Now he was so preoccupied that he scarcely noticed it, and they sat there for some time, she weeping pathetically, he silently thinking while all the anger and resentment and misery drained away, leaving him peaceful and calm.

Eventually, he glanced at the clock. It was well after midnight. Theresa was still whining at the far side of the room, and looked even more grotesque than she had done earlier. He did not know precisely where she lived, and doubted if she knew, either, by this stage. In any case, he decided, he couldn't send her home in such a state, he would have to keep her here. He went over to her side and said, "Come on, Theresa, enough's enough. Time for bed."

He tried to overcome his revulsion: it was like steeling one's nerves to pick up a toad. He moved to touch her sleeve, but she shrank back into the chair. "Come on," he said firmly, and grasped her by the hand. It was clammy and cold. Against her will, he pulled her up out of the chair and dragged her towards the bedroom door, but she began to wriggle and scream until at last he had to manhandle her into the room. As soon as he released his hold she fell to the floor. He pulled the door closed, dashed back to the living-room and gulped down the little that was left of the wine. He hoped she would stay where she was, because he knew that he would not be able to bring himself to touch her again. He marvelled that he had been able to do it at all.

Robert spent the night coiled up uncomfortably on the sofa. For a long time, he could hear Theresa crying in the bedroom with all the venom of an angry baby. Just as he was on the point of dropping off to sleep he thought how desperately confused and distressed she must be; when he put his arm around her waist to heave her into the bedroom, she hadn't even known who he was. Three times she had called him "Francis."

The following morning, he discreetly pretended to be sleeping when he heard the click of the bedroom door. He felt her sweep quickly through the room and he heard the sound of the front door closing. He arose, tidied the flat and spent the rest of the day wondering if it could all have been a strange dream. That night, however, he had sensuous confirmation of its reality, for when he went to bed he found that the pillow and sheets reeked of cigarettes.

"I can't understand how you could do this to me, Theresa, I simply can't understand."

"I'm sorry."

"Sorry's not good enough. After what happened to Francis, if you had thought at all you'd have known that I'd be distracted."

"Look, I said I'm sorry," Theresa snapped. "I can do no more. What do you want, blood?" She had never known it was possible to feel so ill.

"You still haven't said where you were, Theresa," her mother persisted, and Theresa exploded in anger.

"Leave me alone! I'm a grown woman. I'll do as I please and answer to nobody." A wave of nausea succeeded her rage. She ran from the room and spent the rest of the day in bed, feeling angry, guilty, confused, worried and very, very sick.

The following Friday evening, at around 7:00 p.m., Robert's telephone rang.

"Bobby?" said an excited voice.

"Yes, Tom?"

"It's Rosie. She's away in to have it." He was phoning from the Royal Victoria Hospital and said that they had left Tommy with a neighbour. This was part of a pre-arranged plan by which Robert was to collect and mind Tommy until such time as Tom returned, and so, resigning himself to a long night, he gathered together a book, half a bottle of whiskey, a few chocolates with which to bribe his little nephew, and left.

Tommy was tired but excited and Robert had some difficulty in washing, undressing and coaxing him into bed. He had never babysat before, and was indeed so little used to the company of children that he found it distinctly unnerving. It was a great relief when Tommy was at last tucked between the sheets. Even with the child out of sight, however, Robert still felt ill at ease in the tasteless house which had once been his home, and out of the corner of his eye he looked at the things around him: a few scattered, shabby toys; Tom's ashtray, full to overflowing; a crumpled copy of the previous day's *Irish News*, with the form marked in red ink; and an expanding wooden clothes-horse, draped with tiny, damp vests. In the kitchen, his sister's apron hung from a nail, pink, limp and sinister. He always hated being in people's homes and rooms in their absence: it seemed an intrusion. He could never defeat the feeling that the people concerned were really dead and that their dross of belongings was all that remained to make vague, painful, pathetic final statements about them. Sometimes deserted rooms could seem even more artificial, like theatre sets at the end of a play's long run, waiting empty and idle for the stagehands to come and dismantle them.

Every small object in the house seemed a talisman capable of evoking lost souls, and he thought back to the time just after his mother's death when Rosie was attempting to sort through her belongings. Robert had come across his sister sitting on a sheepskin rug in their mother's bedroom, sobbing into an old, torn sweater, which he gently removed from her hands. He sent her down to the kitchen and himself started to sort through the contents of the dressing-table, but it made him unspeakably sad. He felt it was a great affront to her memory as he bundled together the shabby clothes, worn shoes and dingy underwear. He remembered the day she had found the contraceptives in his room and felt very conscious both of being "her son" and of falling far short of what she had thought her son ought to be. He wished that among her effects he might come across something surprising, but he found only things which he might well have expected: broken Rosary beads, a few photographs and old birthday cards, a box of cheap, ginger-coloured face-powder, and a Relic of St. Martin de Porres, which was attached to a large safety-pin. He remembered thinking when he had finished — There: her little soul laid bare before me and I still do not know, I still do not understand.

He watched the late film until the television whined into closedown, and when he unplugged the set he could hear the sound of heavy rain pattering on the pavement. Tommy called for a glass of water, which Robert brought to him. The snout of a grubby Womble protruded over the top of the eiderdown.

"Mammy'll be alright, won't she, Uncle Bobby?"

"Of course," said Robert, thinking of everything that could possibly go wrong, and imagining his sister scream-ing in pain as she bled to death. "Your mammy'll be grand, and then you'll have a new baby sister or brother."

Tommy handed the empty glass back to Robert with a look so full of disbelief and cynicism that his uncle had to restrain himself from saying, "What the hell can you know about childbirth, anyway? You're only five, for God's sake!" Once Robert had told Tommy that there was a fox with big yellow eyes under the bookcase in his flat and Tommy had believed him; and yet when he was told in Bangor to look at the white horses out in the sea he had cried in disappointment because he could see only waves. Robert did not understand children. He went down to the living-room and poured himself a very large whiskey.

He read his book and dozed until 3:30 a.m., when he heard a key being turned in the lock of the front door. Tom had returned.

"It's a wee girl, Bobby," he said, "an' the both of them's

grand. Two of everything down the side an' one of everything down the middle. That's the way it ought to be, isnit? Whiskey! Good man yerself, Bobby!" They filled two tumblers and sat down by the embers of the dying fire. As Tom drank, his buoyancy gradually subsided. He spoke little, and Robert thought that he appeared rather shaken.

"I seen it all, Bobby," he said eventually. "I mean, I knew what it was goin' to be like, and the doctors said there was no problem, but I mean . . . it was rough, Bobby. I mean, it makes ye think." He paused and sipped at his drink. "Yer own wife, Bobby . . . an' then . . . then ye think . . . yer own Ma . . ." He paused again and then gave a nervous and violent sob which startled Bobby, and cried, "I mean, Christ, Bobby, it was fuckin' desprit!" After that there was silence for a long time.

It brought Robert back again to the time of his mother's death, when Rosie's grief had manifested itself primarily as anger. She complained bitterly about every little detail; about the times of the removal of the remains and of the funeral mass; about the body being laid out in the bedroom instead of in the front parlour; about the undertaker's failure to provide a black crepe bow for the front door. Her anger had lingered on afterwards, until the day they attempted to find accurate wording and a suitable verse for the in memoriam cards. In this matter Tom and Rosie looked to Robert for guidance, but their tastes conflicted. Robert liked things literary which his sister found incomprehensible or pagan, or both; so he tried instead for something biblical which would be both religious and nicely phrased, but "The Lord has given and the Lord has taken away; Blessed be the name of Lord" was coldly met by Rosie, who said, "Really, Robert, we're not Presbyterians." For well over an hour they struggled hopelessly to find the words they needed until Rosie at last turned violently on Robert and shouted, "And you're fucking well supposed to be a writer!" All three of them were stunned by this outburst, particularly Rosie. They drifted away from the table without looking at each other. The following day she had handed Robert a torn piece of newspaper and mumbled, "What about this?" Robert read it.

> *Your gentle face and patient smile*
> *With sadness we recall,*
> *You had a kindly word for each,*
> *And died beloved by all.*
> *We miss you now, our hearts are sore,*
> *As time goes by we miss you more.*
> *Your loving smile, your gentle face,*
> *No one can fill your vacant place.*

He handed the paper back to her and said with a little smile, "That'll do fine." She also smiled, understanding that she was forgiven and grateful for that forgiveness: but she did not, and never would, apologise to him, mainly because she had a pathological aversion to apologies, but also because she did not fully realize what she had done. She would never know that her words had cut him to the heart.

Tom gradually became more cheerful, and soon Robert had difficulty in restraining him from going up to wake Tommy and tell him that he had a new baby sister. Before going to bed, he thanked Robert for babysitting. "It's true enough, Bobby, family's what counts at the end of the day."

"Yes," said Robert drily. He tried to really feel this dryness, but he felt instead genuinely sad. Often he wished that he could cut the stick completely with his family, because they had nothing in common, and yet he knew that he would never do it: he valued them too much. The family was like a living souvenir of an age lost and gone. They reminded him of an antique newspaper which shows how much has changed by simple virtue of its price, print, paper, smell, quaintness and the innocence of its news. For he felt that Rosie and Tom were innocents in the way that people were innocents by chronology, with every generation more world-weary than the one before because of the fresh horrors which they have seen. There was something atavistic in Rosie's and Tom's significance to him, and with great reluctance he had to admit that he needed them in his life.

He settled down to another uncomfortable night upon a sofa, and eventually fell asleep thinking about Kathy.

When he arose the following morning, he found father and son already in the kitchen, dishevelled and delighted, taking tea, bap and Weetabix, chattering excitedly about the new baby, spilling things and laughing. Robert filled a mug with tea and wearily watched them. Within a week, Rosie would be home again, bringing with her a new person: not merely new to them, but utterly new. Robert found this a sobering thought. Every day people died and babies were born, but these events only appeared to have cosmic significance when one knew the people involved. Eventually he slipped out to the hall telephone and dialled a Belfast number. He waited for a few moments, then to his joy heard the desired and familiar voice.

"Kathy?"

"Yes."

"It's me, Robert."

"Oh, hello."

"When did you get back?"

"Yesterday."

"Oh. How did you get on in London?"

"Fine. I had a nice time."

"That's good. Listen, Kathy, when can I see you?"

"Well, I'm not really sure now," she demurred.

"Tonight, Kathy. Please." He glanced towards the kitchen door, pressed the receiver closer to his ear and pleaded quietly.

"Please, Kathy. I have to see you. Come to my flat this evening."

"I don't know, Robert . . . I'm not sure . . . Look, leave it with me and I'll see what I can do."

"Great," he said. "Listen, Kathy, I . . ." But she had hung up.

He paused for a moment, then consulted the telephone directory and dialled another Belfast number. Another familiar voice answered.

"Good morning, Theresa," he said smoothly. "Robert here."

There was a long silence. "Theresa?"

"Yes?"

"I just thought you might like to know that my sister had her baby last night. A girl."

"Oh, that's good. I take it they're both well?"

"Yes. She's in the Royal, if you want to see her."

"I might just do that. Thanks." There was another silence, which he waited vainly for her to fill, and at last he said insinuatingly, "Kathy's back from London."

"Yes, I know."

This piqued him and he again waited in silence, but she evidently shared Rosie's aversion to apologies. He wondered if she remembered coming to his flat, then decided that she was bound to. He considered saying to her bluntly, "Did you get home alright the other morning?" but glanced again at the kitchen door and thought better of it. "Well, that's the score, anyway," he said lamely.

"Right. Well, thanks for phoning. Goodbye." She hung up.

Under his breath Robert comprehensively cursed all women, replaced the receiver and returned to the kitchen.

In Boots' baby department, Theresa dithered over bears, rugs, pandas, shawls and tiny hats. The longer she looked, the less able she was to decide, and if an elderly woman had not eventually pointed to the Baby-Gros and said, "Great yokes, thon', wish we'd had them when mine were wee," she might never have clinched it, might have wandered off in despair and bought chocolates.

It was four days after Robert's telephone call that Theresa at last mustered the courage and energy to go visit Rosie in hospital. It was to the Royal that Francis's body had been brought for identification, and she had not been back to it since that time. She feared hospitals with a primitive and childish fear. This was where strange people "did" things to you. This was where people's bodies, vulnerable at the best of times, were at their weakest and most pitiful. Everything possible was done in hospitals to maintain life, and still people died.

On reaching the ward, she peeped timidly around the door, afraid that Robert would be there. It was a relief to see Rosie's familiar face amidst the anonymous iron bedsteads, the flowers, cards, Lucozade and grapes; and she was pleased to note that there was no one with her. Rosie was delighted to see Theresa, and proudly handed the baby to her. It fitted snugly in her embrace, and suddenly Theresa felt that she had been waiting unconsciously all that summer, all her life, for that moment when she would take the baby in her arms and feel the perfection of its weight, shape and warmth; as if the baby had been created uniquely for that moment and for her arms.

"Robert thinks it's a dote," said Rosie, "but he's not the sort as would say." Theresa did not answer. The baby wrinkled its face, pressed its tongue between its gum and lower lip and yawned lazily. Its eyes were deep, dark and unseeing, and Theresa thought: the worst fate this child might have would not be to end up like Francis, but to end up like me. Rosie and her baby made love look simple and normal. Theresa wished that it were so and then thought: perhaps it is. Perhaps it is for everyone except me. What if my body were at this moment drained of all blood and pigment, until I became transparent as glass? Then they would see through to my cold, black, hidden heart, and I would be banished at once from this warm and tender room. Feeling unworthy, she sadly handed the baby back to its mother.

Rosie prattled on happily about Tom and Tommy and the baby while Theresa struggled to keep smiling. She had not thought that the visit would be so deeply traumatic, and she left as soon as she decently could. On crossing the hallway, she saw Robert enter the building and was obliged to dart behind a pillar to avoid him. She could not believe that she had had such a narrow escape. Rosie and a baby had been difficult. Rosie and Robert and a baby would have been impossible.

As he walked across the hallway, unconscious that he was being watched, Robert thought how glad he would be when Rosie at last went home, for then he would no longer have to visit the hospital. His mother had died there, and returning to this place had brought that time back to him in a way which he would never have believed possible. The freshness of his memories shocked him. He had forgotten so much, both of the events and the emotions: now he was forced to live through them all again.

Their mother had remained conscious for less than a day after her admission, then slipped into a deep coma which had lasted for three more days. Days? They had exploded time; he and Rosie had neither eaten nor slept while day seeped into night seeped into day; unending, nightmarish; until all terms to express time became meaningless. He thought that he could remember a life which had been lived out somewhere else, in houses, libraries, pubs and bookshops, and began to wonder if it was a dream or a hallucination, for he felt that he had been and would be in that cramped and overheated room for all eternity. He could not believe that there was a world other than this: Rosie, red-eyed, holding her mother's hand to ensure that the small crucifix which she had tucked into the dying woman's slack fist remained there; and a respirator wheezing and clicking in the corner, as if it were the one dying, rather than the still, frail woman upon the sterile bed. She had been connected up to a heart monitor and they had blankly watched the brilliant green line of light wiggle across the black screen, while little numbers clicked in the corner, high and steady, until a few hours before the end. He had felt at one stage a wave of unexpected anger well up in him, and thought, "If she can't live, why doesn't she die and have done with it?" He wanted to, and was afraid that he would, move quickly forward and pull all the wires and tubes from her body, rip all the machines from their sockets and so get all three of them out of this horror, push the entire family over the brink into grief and release. It was the first time he had experienced coming to the absolute limits of his endurance, only to find that he had to drag himself on past those limits. He had never known that it was possible to suffer so much and still be alive.

The numbers on the screen had dropped swiftly towards the end. When they clicked to double-zero and the green line became straight, Robert and Rosie turned quickly to each other, and each saw in the other's eyes disbelief and shock.

He walked through the door of the maternity ward. Rosie looked up from the baby and smiled at him.

"Guess who you've just missed?" she said.

Kathy did not keep her appointment with Robert, broke another engagement three days later, and it was almost a week after her return when she at last deigned to go to his flat. The meeting was a disaster from the moment he opened the door and said, "Welcome back. How was the family reunion?"

"Who told you about that?" she said angrily.

"Theresa," he replied. "I didn't know that it was supposed to be a secret. I can't see why it should be."

"And when were you talking to Theresa?"

Robert began to relate the whole story of her visit and the more he talked the more he wished that he had kept silent. Kathy glowered angrily throughout, although he tried to tell his tale lightly, making it a thing insignificant and amusing. Kathy did not laugh. When he had finished she said, "This is all news to me. I've seen Theresa three times since I got back and she didn't say anything about it."

"Do you wonder?" he exclaimed with a giggle of desperate mirth. "It doesn't show her in a very good light."

"It's not much to your credit, either."

"I don't know what you can mean," he said stiffly. "She came of her own accord and half-plastered. I didn't want her; I thought she was a right pest. She was lucky I didn't throw her out on her ear five minutes after she arrived."

"Such kindness and charity," Kathy sneered defensively.

London had confused her. At first she had felt a union with her father and his family, and had delighted in their casual lives. The elder of the two girls strongly resembled Kathy and had many of her mannerisms; her father's second wife, Sophie, was young and friendly. But, as the days went on, a feeling of alienation crept over her. All the little things which distanced her from the family gradually became more obvious. She became increasingly conscious of the children's English accents, so different to her own; and of the fact that they were only half-sisters. One day, as a joke, Kathy referred to Sophie as her stepmother, and both of them immediately realized that it was the truth. From that moment on, they were never completely comfortable in each other's company. Gradually, she admitted to herself that she was not one of the family: it was her father's family, but it was not hers.

The night before she was due to come home, she lay awake in bed thinking of all the little failures and inadequacies of the trip; of all the moments when a word or a look had proved to her (although without malice) that she was only a visitor, and she had been seized with a sudden craving for a family life, a life of her own. She knew all the difficulties and drawbacks, but still she wanted it. Now she was glad that she had not told cynical old Robert why she was going to London. He would have laughed, she thought, if she told him this. He set little store by his own family; he would never understand. As soon as she arrived in Belfast, she missed her father and the family so much that she could hardly bear it. She could not talk about her loneliness, and so translated it into anger. Robert and Theresa had unwittingly given her a convenient target for this anger.

Robert watched her, and knew that Theresa had been right. Kathy had changed; and he worried about the consequences.

September arrived, damp and cold, and Theresa thought with dread of the coming winter. It would bring Francis's second anniversary, the horrors of Christmas, with all its maudlin sentimentality and aggressive bonhomie, followed by the New Year, which she always found unspeakably sad. She did not understand how people could celebrate the passage of time. January: the dead of winter. She would have to drag herself somehow through the dark, dreary months of the young year, until spring came, with Easter, green shoots and the first shred of hope.

She seriously wondered if this time she would have the stamina to make it through to March, for it seemed a lifetime away.

Feeling wilful and trapped, Theresa knelt in church before the crucifix, remembering how, when it was veiled in Lent, it had looked like a kite of purple silk. Once, during the unveiling on Good Friday, the priest had dropped one of the elastic bands which held the silk in place, and she had seen it lying on the carpet as she knelt at the altar rails, a long, fine, gum-coloured lemniscate. The stuff of religious symbols was so paltry and mundane: paper and stone and metal and wood and wax; but perhaps this purple veil upon a cross was the best symbol possible. Silk stretched over wood; a symbol concealing a symbol. Things of importance and truth were always layered and hidden. When Francis died, they had placed him in a coffin with a small chrome crucifix fixed to the lid; and she remembered looking at it and knowing that she would never again be afraid to die. In Russia, his coffin would have been carried open to the graveside, but they had not been permitted to see his poor dead face and cold forehead. She remembered tenderly stroking the wood of the coffin and trying to visualize his dear, broken body within. She imagined his features sharpened in death, sharper, sharper to corruption, and then she knew why medieval knights and lords had had statues carved or wrought to represent their own bodies, and placed upon their tombs. These people of marble and bronze were first an image of the body which lay beneath, but soon became a dishonest distraction, attempting to belie the hidden bones and dust. White sepulchres. Futility. His coffin had been carried for a short distance and then placed in the hearse. Theresa and her mother had found themselves looking at their own reflections, ghostly and bloodless as photographic negatives, cast upon the glass behind which lay the solid coffin and a few bright wreaths of flowers.

She wondered why she worried the memory of his death again and again, like a dog with a bone, for she felt that the death itself was not at the heart of her distress. When she watched his burial, it was as if the gravediggers were tucking him up for the rest of time with a thick brown blanket, living and warm and moist. She knew that in springtime his grave would be greened over with grasses and weeds, and she believed that her brother was now perfected. Too late she wished that she had jumped in with him, so that the gravediggers could cover up the living and dead together: she longed for the soft, damp soil to muffle her ears and gag her mouth, to seal her eyes up in union and death.

Months later, she had scribbled on a scrap of paper, "I loved him too much," then tossed it into the fire and watched it burn.

"Do you reject Satan?"
"I do."
"And all his works?"
"I do."
"And all his empty promises?"

"I do."

"Do you believe in God, the Father almighty, creator of Heaven and earth?"

"I do."

Robert listened as the sacramental words dropped into the still, cold air of the church. It gave him a curious sensation, as if he were attending not a baptism in West Belfast, but a primitive and mysterious religious ceremony in a gloomy, subterranean temple, far distant in both time and space from the reality he knew. That reality was a late Sunday afternoon in September, and already the darkness was pressing lightly against the windows, draining all colour and so making it difficult to distinguish the saints and symbols depicted in the stained glass. At the top of the church there was a rectangular candelabra, where numerous little discs of white wax were ranged in tiers, their flames waving, guttering and making the air all around them glow, while down at the back, where the font stood, there was little light save from a single candle which Tom's brother was holding in his capacity as godfather. Its flame cast ghastly and sinister shadows upon the faces of those gathered around, and as the bright baptismal water sparkled across the baby's forehead it caught the light of the candle. The child did not cry, but Robert could see its little feet working frantically beneath the shawl.

Theresa was kneeling almost directly opposite Robert, her eyes closed and her head bowed in prayer. With a jolt, he thought: "She really believes in this. They all do." They believed that mere water and words and all this theatrical mumbo-jumbo had the power to free the baby from the grip of evil. They believed that this ceremony was absolutely vital for the well-being of the child. They spoke of the Devil as if he were lurking behind a nearby pillar. Robert tried to imagine the Devil, and saw him as tall, thin and blood-red, with thick, black hair and cold, dark eyes. He saw the Devil toy thoughtfully with the barb at the end of his long, slimy tail and take particular care to stand very still, lest his cloven hooves be heard to rattle upon the stone floor of the church. Robert felt a nervous giggle rise in his throat, and he bowed his head.

But what if it all were true? God and the Devil. Sin and death. Heaven and Hell. What if this water and light really meant something? What if there were four last things to be remembered instead of just one? He raised his eyes and looked at the little group before him. Try as he might, he found it impossible to understand, or imagine, or empathize with, their belief, and because of this inability he thought that belief must make a huge difference to the way one saw life — saw everything. It was little wonder that he had had such difficulty with his mother, or that he could not understand Rosie or Theresa. Even Kathy would admit, under pressure, that she believed in God. Robert's closest approach to faith in the last ten years had been when he looked at his mother's dead body and found that he could not believe that what he saw was in any significant way the person he had known. More importantly, he could not believe that she was nowhere, that she was simply gone, annihilated. He felt that she must be somewhere, but he could not begin to imagine where; could never have dared to define or name the state or place where his mother now was. Suddenly he understood the drift of his thoughts, and his mind balked in horror. It implied too much for him, and filled him with dread. She is dead, he told himself, dead, dead, dead.

Now, in church, he remembered that moment, and felt pity for believers. The priest talked about evil, and Robert felt afraid. He wished that he had not come. The wax of the candle steadily dripped.

They all went back to Rosie's and Tom's house after the christening, as Rosie had prepared a small buffet, the centrepiece of which was a large fruit cake coated in royal icing and garnished with a pink plastic stork. Robert ensured that Theresa was well supplied with tea, ham sandwiches and sausage rolls, then edged her into a corner and was surprised to find himself bluntly asking, "Theresa, do you really believe in all that mumbo-jumbo?"

"The christening? Why, yes, of course I do. I wouldn't have been there otherwise."

"But don't you find it . . . medieval? I mean, it's so . . . so creepy."

"In what way?" she asked, nibbling on a sandwich.

"Well, for example, what has a little baby got to do with sin and evil and the Devil?"

"Rather a lot, I should think, seeing that said baby has been doomed by birth to life in Belfast," she said drily. "Don't try to tell me that there's no evil in this city just because you can't see a Devil with cloven hooves wandering around."

"Is that what the Devil looks like, then?"

"How should I know? He probably looks like lots of things. He might look a bit like you, who can say?" She smirked and wiped some crumbs from the corner of her mouth. He ignored the insult and persisted with his interrogation.

"But why are you a Christian, Theresa?"

She shrugged and said, "Because it's a good religion for me."

"But why?"

She gave a deep sigh and replied in a soft voice, "Because it's the religion for victims and failures. It's for people who are diseased and depraved. It's for people who are subversive; who can detect and denounce evil even when it looks comfortable and respectable, and particularly when it's in their own hearts and minds. People who can see below the surface of things, and who have difficulty in accepting their own existence. But I'm not answering your question, am I?"

"Aren't you?"

"No. There's only one valid reason for believing in Christianity."

"And what's that?"

"Because it's the truth. I mean, you can't be a Christian just because you find it an attractive notion, or because it seems comfortable — you soon find out that it's not that, anyway. Nor can you do it for the sake of beauty, because it has too much to do with the ugly, broken side of life. You do it because you have to. If you know that Christianity is the truth, then you have no choice but to be a Christian."

Robert listened and was lost. He felt as if there were a thick wall of glass between himself and Theresa, for in no way could he relate to what she was saying. It was like hearing someone defending the flat-earth theory, or soberly claiming that they had once caught a unicorn.

"What's the point of it all, then?" he asked. "Does it make you happy?"

"No. Maybe it's not supposed to. Maybe I'm not a very good Christian. In any case, you do it for God, not for what's in it for yourself. But it does do one thing: it allows you to live with your own conscience. It means that you're at least trying to live with integrity; you know that you're struggling in the right direction . . ." She fell silent and looked away, for she could not find words to express the tensions which lay between faith and the "however" side of life. Robert could not know what it was like to glimpse perfection and know that that was the state to which one had to aspire, only suddenly to see it offset by the immense imperfection of one's self. She could not explain how weary it made her to know that she would never be good enough.

"I want to go home."

She said goodbye to Rosie and Tom and thanked them for their hospitality. Robert insisted on walking at least part of the way home with her, and together they set off up the Falls Road. It was twilight. His mother had fallen ill on just such an evening. They had followed the ambulance down to the hospital by car, and on the way he had seen three young girls in pale summer dresses run lightly along the pavement. They had seemed like wraiths in the dusk, and he remembered thinking, "They are not real and so none of this can be reality. This is a dream from which I will soon awaken."

Theresa remained silent as they walked. Both were conscious that some reference ought to be made to Kathy, but neither of them could bring themselves to do it. Robert glanced at Theresa and thought it weird that someone could be so near to him and yet so distant in mind and heart. Eventually she said, "This is where I live, goodnight." He watched while she crossed the road to a high, red-brick terrace, and watched until the home at the end of the row had swallowed her up in blackness.

Robert sat at his desk in the library, browsing through a large leather-bound volume of newspapers. Although they were less than two years old, they smelt musty and sour. He turned the yellowed pages with great care to avoid tearing them.

Kathy had arrived at his flat the preceding evening, bringing with her all the books which she borrowed from him in the course of the summer, and had never before troubled to return. He found this ominous. He made coffee while she sat down in the wicker chair where Theresa had sat during her unexpected visit, and when Robert came in from the kitchen with the tray he was annoyed to see her choice of seat, for it was ostentatiously distant from the corner where he habitually sat. He poured out the coffee and put a record on the stereo. She asked politely about his book and he said that it was almost completed. Kathy took a small notebook from her handbag and scribbled something down, then tore out the page and handed it to Robert. "That's a play to which you ought to refer. It was first produced in Belfast. You should check it out. Get the reviews from the local papers; they'll have them in the library. I think you'll find it interesting." Robert looked at the page. He had never heard of either the play or the author before. Kathy had also conveniently added the date of production. "Thank you," he said.

Their subsequent conversation was sparse, for they had nothing left to say to each other. Robert wondered why it always had to end like this, with a steady drifting to indifference and silence. As night fell, he could see the ghostly room begin to crystallize behind the dark glass, and the clearer it became the more it unsettled him. At last he went over to the window and lowered the blinds. As he passed behind Kathy's chair on the way back, he stopped and tentatively stroked the back of her neck. She swore and jerked her head aside as if she had been stung. "I beg your pardon," he said very coldly. Hurt and angry, he crossed to the stereo.

"I think we ought to have a change of music, don't you? What about this one, it's perfect, it's called, 'I Used to Love Her But It's All Over Now.' "

Kathy stood up. "Very amusing, Robert," she said. "But not quite accurate. You never loved me. But you're right about its being over." She picked up her coat and left the room. Robert did not follow and from where he stood he could hear the front door close behind her.

As he thumbed through the faded newspapers the following day, he felt sad. He doubted that the reviews would be significant, or even relevant, but he felt that he had to find them as a final and token gesture to Kathy. At last he came to the issue for the given date, and began to scan the columns carefully. The first two pages revealed nothing, and when he turned over the third frail page he saw a large grainy photograph of Theresa. Startled, he read the caption. "Miss Theresa Cassidy at the funeral yesterday of her twin brother, Francis." He quickly read the accompanying report, which dealt mainly with the funeral, but revealed to Robert that Francis had been murdered. He then rapidly turned back to the issues for the days immediately preceding. The report of three days before said that the badly mutilated body of a young man had been found on a patch of waste ground near the city centre. By the following day he had been identified and his name released: Francis Cassidy, 21, a Roman Catholic who had no connections with the security forces or with any paramilitary organization. He had been abducted on his way to work in a supermarket near the city centre. The murder was described as "particularly brutal" and the motive appeared to be purely sectarian. There was a small photograph of the dead man, who looked so like Theresa that Robert shivered.

The discovery stunned and confused him, and he did not know what to think. Foolishly, he tried to remember what he had been doing around that date two years ago, as if that knowledge could help him to understand or control in some way this dreadful new reality. He could not recall the murder from papers or news reports which he might have heard or read at that time. It had been a particularly brutal and cruel killing, but it was still only one out of so many hundreds of brutal and cruel killings. He looked up at the people around him in the library, reading and writing and browsing and whispering. It shocked him to think of the evils and sorrows which might be in their minds and hearts: no one could see or guess the things which they might have done or endured. He looked down again at the photograph of Francis, and was suddenly conscious of someone standing close behind him. He quickly raised his head, and saw to his horror that it was Theresa, who at that very moment glanced down casually over his shoulder at the book laid open before him. She saw Francis's photograph and her face changed immediately, becoming pale and impassive as a mask. Without saying a word, she turned and walked away. Robert watched her go, and could have wept with embarrassment. He did not know what to do. He could not bring himself to go after her, and in any case he was not sure if that was what the situation required.

Attempting to avert his eyes from the photograph, he closed the heavy volume and returned it to the issue desk, but waited for a long time before leaving the library.

Three times that afternoon, Robert tried to phone Theresa, but each time there was no reply. By late evening he had decided that meeting her again would be so awkward and embarrassing that he wanted to do it as soon as possible and get it over. He therefore drove over to West Belfast and parked outside the house which he had seen her enter on the day of the christening. A light glowed in the bay window. Timidly, he knocked upon the door, and as soon as Theresa opened it he felt that he had compounded his error by coming to her home. He wished that he could garble out upon the doorstep all he had to say and then run, but he had the wit to know that to attempt this would be the final and greatest insult.

"Oh," said Theresa when she saw him. She had a few pound notes in her left hand. "I thought you were the paper boy."

"May I come in?"

"Of course," she said, but seemed annoyed, and he did not know if this was because she did not really want him to enter; or because she had intended to usher him in anyway, and the request to be admitted was thus an insult to her hospitality. Feeling wretched, he followed her into a dim hallway, and on through into a small parlour.

"I hope I'm not intruding," he mumbled.

"Not at all," said Theresa, indicating a chair by the fireside. "You owe me a visit." He sat down and felt slightly more at ease than he had done on the doorstep. Theresa remained standing. On the wall behind her was a round mirror surrounded by a garland of leaves wrought from black metal. Robert gazed thankfully past Theresa's head into the glass, where he could see the whole room reflected, circular and small, distorted at the circumference because of the mirror's convexity. It reminded him of a painting — what was it called? — "The Arnolfini Marriage," was that it? Robert could see himself in the mirror as if he were the artist who had created all before him, both the room and the room reflected. He remembered from the painting trivial domestic details — a little dog; some oranges; a pair of slippers carelessly tossed aside — and as he thought this he noticed that Theresa was wearing the most absurd bedroom slippers he had ever seen: a pair of mules which engulfed her feet in two clouds of candy-pink imitation fur. Had he not seen them for himself, he would never have believed her guilty of possessing such things.

"When you've finished gazing into the middle distance," she suddenly drawled, "you might speak to me."

"I'm sorry," he blurted out, and wished that he could escape into the circular reflected room, or that he really were a figure in a painting, with the crabbed inscription "Johannes de dyck fuit hic" upon the flock wallpaper, to prove the artifice. "I'm sorry about what happened this morning."

"Next time you're checking someone out like that, Robert, remember to sit facing the door."

"But I wasn't checking you out. Honestly, Theresa, I came upon that report when I was looking for something else. It was pure coincidence . . ."

She raised an eyebrow cynically, knelt down by the

fire and lit a cigarette from a small ember which she plucked from the grate with the tongs. "Funny coincidence," she said, sitting back on her heels.

"I tell you, it's the truth. I was looking for a play review — look, I can even tell you the name of it." He took from his pocket the crumpled page which Kathy had given to him, and passed it to Theresa. She glanced at it indifferently, then looked again more closely.

"But this is Kathy's handwriting."

"Yes," he said, "Kathy gave me the reference to check. She said that it was important."

Theresa looked back at the page, then suddenly to Robert's amazement her eyes filled up with tears and she said bitterly, "She may have found her father, but she's still her mother's daughter."

"Theresa," said Robert wearily, "I give up. I know that I probably ought to understand all this, but it's beyond me."

"For someone who's supposed to be educated, Robert, you can be very dense. But tell me this: did someone as *au fait* with the theatre in Belfast as yourself not find it strange that a significant play was produced here less than two years ago and yet you had never heard of either author or play? And when you couldn't find the reviews, did you not think it odder still?"

"How do you know that I didn't find them?"

"You tell me, Robert. Yes, Robert, yes," she said, seeing sudden understanding in his face. "That's the way it is. Sweet girl, Kathy, isn't she?"

"But why did she do it?"

"To hurt me. To get her revenge because I went to see you when she was in London, and because I told you about her father. She doesn't need or want us now that she has her precious Daddy and sisters."

"Does it matter so much that I know about your brother?"

"Yes," she said shortly. There had been a time when she had wanted everyone to know, when she had craved pity: look at me, look at how much I have to suffer. She wanted her suffering to frighten others as much as it frightened herself. That time had passed, leaving inexplicable feelings of shame, as if she were somehow tainted by his murder. She felt guilty for continuing to live while he was dead, and the pity of others now sickened her, for under it she saw contempt. "It matters a lot. It matters to me."

Robert tried to visualize the dead boy at home in this cosy room: curled up in a fat armchair; kneeling at the tiled hearth or looking at his reflection in the circular mirror, but his imagination failed him. Francis remained one of those grey people (and his own father was another) whose existence, Robert knew, could be proven, but whose reality he could never quite grasp. "You have to get over these things," he said with a hint of impatience. "Surely your religion must give you some comfort?" She turned on him, more angry than he had ever before seen her.

"Comfort? Why do you miserable atheists always say that about religion? You don't know what it's like to suffer and believe. Where's the comfort in knowing that God Himself had to die because of my sins? Where's the comfort in knowing that I'll never be good enough? Where's the comfort in trying to escape suffering when I know that I ought to cherish it? You're the one who has it easy, because you don't believe in sin or in judgment. You think that when you die there'll be blackness and silence and nothing. You don't believe that you'll ever need forgiveness for all the evil things you've done, and that makes you dangerous. It was people who thought that they were above forgiveness that killed my brother."

"But you believe that your brother's in Heaven now, don't you? You believe that he's at peace?"

"Yes, but what about me?" she cried. "What about me? I loved Francis as dearly as I loved my own life, but he was taken from me and tortured and killed. I have to go on living without him, and I have to go on believing in God, a good God, a God who loves and cares for me. Do you think that's easy? I have to believe that my brother's death was a victory. I have to forgive the people who killed my brother; I have to try to love them as I loved him. I have to try to think of *them* as brothers while in my heart I want to hate them: and then you dare to speak to me of comfort? You tell me what's easy about belief. You tell me where the comfort is."

She was crying long before she ceased to speak, and continued to cry in the following silence. Robert listened to her, remembering how he had once heard her weeping far into the night on the other side of his closed bedroom door. He was awed not by the depth of her faith, but by the intransigence of her will, seeing in her a refusal to be comforted as staunch as his own refusal to believe. He remembered his mother making much of God's mercy and grace, but he did not dare mention it. He wished that he could take her in his arms and weep, too, but his usual revulsion for her body was now compounded with fear, for he felt that if he were to touch her, all that immense anger and grief would thrill through him like electricity and he would be brought down to suffer there with her. Her professedly comfortless faith did do something: it made her grief finite; but he felt that if he were to fall he would fall forever and forever.

"Leave me," she sobbed. "Please go away and leave me."

Robert wanted to speak but could find nothing to say. Feeling wretched, he quietly left the room and her home. As soon as he had gone, Theresa slid to the rug and lay there crying with a total lack of restraint until she was spent and could cry no more. She wondered how long she had been lying there in tears: perhaps for half an hour, perhaps for even longer. Sniffing pathetically, she curled up on the rug until she could touch her feet, then removed a slipper, smelt it and stroked its soft, synthetic fur against her damp face while gazing at the dusty grey cinders of the fire. She thought of nothing.

After a long time, she heard a single knock upon the front door. She waited, listened and heard a second knock. Raising herself to her knees, she listened again, and when the third knock came she arose and went into the hall. As soon as she saw Theresa's face in the ghastly yellow light of the street lamp, Kathy knew that she had come too late.

"Robert's been here, hasn't he?" she said. "Oh, Theresa . . ." She stepped into the house, but would go no further than the tiny porch formed between the main house door and a light inner door inset with a square pane of glass into which was frosted the image of a bowl of roses. Only a very little light filtered through from the hall and the street by way of the frosted glass and the fanlight: the porch remained dim. "I told him in such a roundabout way that afterwards I thought: he won't find out or if he does he won't mention it; it doesn't matter. But all day today I couldn't get Francis out of my mind and I thought, of course it matters, of course it's important. I could hardly believe that I had done such a thing, and I couldn't forgive myself. Can you forgive me?"

"Yes," said Theresa's voice in the darkness. "Of course I forgive you."

"I feel so bad about this," said Kathy. "It's dreadful to do something wrong, and then know that absolutely nothing can undo it."

"Kathy, I've forgiven you," said Theresa wearily. "I can do nothing more."

"I'm sorry, Theresa. I'm really, really sorry. Look, I'll leave you now because you're tired, but I promise I'll phone tomorrow. Goodnight. And thanks."

"Goodnight."

Kathy left and Theresa returned to the parlour. She reached for the cigarette packet but found it empty; swore and folded her arms in frustration. Then she caught sight of her reflection in the round mirror, and was startled. Who was that person? Could that pale, hunched, ugly little person be herself? She could scarcely believe how intimately she must know the sad hinterland of the red-eyed girl's life, and she approached the mirror timidly, watching with fascination the way in which the image grew. Stopping before it, she was filled with a desire to touch the glass. She remembered when she was a child at school a priest had once come to show slides of the Missions, and halfway through the showing she and Francis had risen, with a shared, single impulse, and run across the dark room together to stroke the wall, believing that the bright pictures being cast upon it would magically change its texture. (Francis said afterwards to the angry teacher, "I wanted to feel what Africa was like.") Of course they were disappointed when their touch encountered only the ordinary wall; but they did distort the image: they did have the satisfaction of seeing the African veldt at dusk ripple across their tiny hands, even if they could not feel it.

Stretching up, she touched the mirror with the tips of her fingers. It was, of course, cold and smooth. What else, even now, did she expect? She withdrew her hand and gazed again at her reflection. Me. The metal leaves framed her as she stood, still and dead as a painting. Could there be anything more wearisome, she wondered, than to stand alone, alone, alone before a mirror? How long would it be, she wondered, until she could go beyond reflections? For how long would she have to continue claiming the face in the mirror as her own? When would there be an end to shadows cast upon glass?

Theresa turned her back upon the mirror, with its cold, circular, distorted room, and looked around the real parlour in which she was standing. She realized that she was very cold. Shivering, she crossed to the hearth, knelt down and tried to rekindle the dying fire.